Tales
from
GRIMMGARD

TODD MIKA

Todd Mika

EDITED BY STEPHANIE LIEBER & AMY FRANTZ

Thank you for reading!

First edition December 2020

Cover Art by David "Huffychip" Smith

Tales from Grimmgard

ISBN-13 978-0-9909319-1-1 (Paperback Edition)

https://www.grimmgard.com/

TABLE OF CONTENTS

"I saw the very dawn of lifekind itself. I saw the reins of the mortal world change hands from the Titans of old to these foolish, petty, squabbling children. I have set in motion purposes fulfilled not by a single mortal life, but his son and his son's son, to the fifth generation. They are born, they live, they die. They are like leaves on a tree, little sparrow. They fall, and they grow again. We do not weep for the fallen leaves."

~Oczandarys, Prince of Angelics

DESTRUCTION

C hasmira was nearly knee-deep in the mire. Her leggings and the hem of her dress were caked in green-black muck.

Across the moonlit bog, she could see Hakon. His unmistakable black, pointed, pyramidal helmet rose like a spike. She heard the rumble of primordial force and a brief scream echoing.

These two had faced a hundred footsoldiers thus far. More would come.

Four hours ago, the two stood on opposite ends of a battlefield. Chasmira was dark seer to Magnate Argolvrecht and the scarlet-armored warriors that flowed like blood from a wound, out the gates of Dimol Gol. Hakon was grand executor for the Mad Prince Mirikinin and his hordes of hooded barbarians that bore spiked shields and saw-toothed warblades.

Argolvrecht was dead — torn to bits by Mirikinin's ironwolves. Mirikinin was also dead — skewered by a flurry of Dimol Gol arrows. There was no point in fighting when neither kingdom existed any longer. But the soldiers fought anyway, neither side knowing their lord was gone. When the battlefield cleared, there wouldn't be enough standing warriors to lay siege to a chicken farm.

So they walked. The two sorcerers, through the marshland, making their way south and away from the battlefield. Deserters of a pointless war, and treated as deserters.

The chittering song of insects went quiet. Chasmira heard a burbling war cry as a hooded barbarian, covered in dark mud, leapt from under the water! His sword was raised to cleave her in two. Flames kindled in her eyes, but with a bright white flash and a roar of primordial force, the barbarian shattered like pottery before the seer could act.

"Art thou weary?" Hakon chuckled in a deep bass tone. The executor was like a wall of angular black armor over eight feet tall. He raised his iron staff back into an upright position at his side. Its three-pronged tip was still steaming.

The flames in her eyes dwindled back into their perpetual glow, each eye with a candle's flicker behind the pupil. "No, curious. I was wondering if he'd actually strike a lady unprovoked. Mirikinin's men have no manners at all."

"Nay, none. Like unto animals, all of them."

"You say that as if you disapprove of them. Are you of noble birth yourself, Hakon?"

"Thou art a jester."

"I felt like one these past six months, believe me." Entertaining Magnate Argolvrecht's mad ravings required a gentle hand and a generous amount of patience. Most of the time, her warnings were drowned in a court filled with bloodlusted barbarians. She was little more than another trinket in a trophy case, displayed to make him look impressive. "Confess. Whose courtier was your mother?"

Hakon scoffed, "Do wild boars of these very lands hold court?"

"You're kidding," she cackled, but only once so as not to wound him. "You were born here... Here, in these stinking pits?"

"Yea, a century ago, these marshlands were very fair. Feeding grounds for wild boars. Nomadic hunters did hunt and pitch here."

"How did they teach you the Arts?"

"They? Nay, not at all. When my powers did manifest, the hunters brought me to the Phrontistery of First Fire."

That was a name Chasmira had not heard in a very long time. Trudging in the thick mire, she stumbled. Her ankle had caught on a tree root for a moment. She caught herself, cursed, and placed her steps more carefully.

"The Sorcerers of the White Aegis didn't drop from the sky and into your hunting grounds?" she asked him.

"The White Aegis careth not to foster the weak. They descend where Chaos threatens, where it doth grow and then sprout out of young, rebellious hearts. For what cause doth one summon Chaos in their youth, but to destroy and control that which standeth in the way? It is this strength of spirit that draweth the White Aegis. They have crafted purposes for such, but not for someone such as myself."

"You, weak of spirit? I could hardly imagine, Hakon."

The compliment bounced off Hakon. "Thy power didst not draw the eyes of the White Aegis? Did they not send one of their own to find thee?"

"They did, actually."

"And?"

Chasmira rolled her eyes at the towering Hakon. "They should have sent two and not underestimated a little girl."

"Verily. Thy family should have brought thee to the Phrontistery as well."

"They might have if even one soul of them were left."

For a long minute after, the only exchange was the crackle of vines and squelching of mud as the two of them continued on without a word.

"Thy tale is befitting the long, dark road ahead," the towering executor said, breaking the silence. "Start with your birthplace, so that we may have enough words to match our steps."

"Ohh, now, now! We are companions of convenience. Don't fancy any thoughts that you and I will be bosom-friends when this is over and done. We'll eventually find the road that leads to Argismora—"

"Argismora? The Guardian City?"

"Yes and why not?"

"Thinkest thou—"

A loud clang sounded from Hakon's armor as a Dimol Gol arrow bounced off it. Chasmira turned, and a long stream of bright flame shot from her eyes into the cattails on her left. The scream of the archer was brief but shrill.

"Thinkest I—?" she prompted, blinking away fire.

"Thinkest thou, that thou shalt go to serve another lord? Thy reputation doth win thee easy hire."

"It is likely. The life of a courtier suits me. Even if I cannot sit upon a throne of power myself, the view from beside one is enchanting," she said, stepping over a log.

Hakon stepped onto the log and it snapped in half. "Thou sayest. But methinkest thy desires are contrary one to another."

"Why would you say such a thing?"

"Because thy reputation doth not agree with thee. The view beside a throne is splendid indeed, but better befitting a pillar or a gargoyle. Thy mind is nought. Thy words are nought if all thou doest is agree. Wilt thou never rouse another up to let thee be heard?"

"No, I don't think I ever will."

"Why not?"

"Because I deny myself the vanity of fancying things that will never be." She heard a noise, and hot streams of golden fire burst forth again. Clumps of ashes scattered across the bog, flickering in the heat. Stinking steam rose from the spot. She didn't even notice whether it was crimson armor or a black hood this time.

~

The bog eventually gave way to a road. It was man-made, insomuch as firm earth had been moved and reinforced with large stones to create a rise several feet above the steaming mire. The lumpy, moss-covered road snaked its way through the boglands, but one could not tell north from south. Neither sun nor sky could be seen, for the land was choked with vines and gnarled trees. Hakon and Chasmira looked one way, and then the other.

"Which way?" the woman mused aloud.

"Betwixt the two of us, thou art the one going to Argismora. Thou knowest not thy way?"

She considered lashing him with fire from her eyes as she glared back at him. "I don't often detour through the stinking, pig-infested bog on my way to the main road, no. I'm not sure which way to go."

"We knowwww!" a choir of high-pitched voices shouted from the bog!

Hakon whirled about, bringing his iron staff down into both hands and aiming it at the source of the outburst! The three prongs at the forked tip thrummed loudly with a rush of primordial power, ready to destroy! His grip went a little slack, however, when he saw he was pointing it at a cluster of mushrooms growing between the stones of the roadside.

"Couldn't be..."

The mushrooms tittered and giggled, with tiny black eyes peeking open beneath their bulbs. It sounded like babies' laughter, and Hakon did not even draw back his staff from the surprise.

Chasmira tip-toed off the road and knelt on the mossy hillside. Lifting Hakon's staff gently away with the back of her hand, she spoke to the cluster of tiny creatures.

"Why hello down there! Did you say you know the way?"

The mushrooms giggled again, and all began to chatter at once. They were Cloven: tiny, endlessly playful little things who began life in clustered patches like these. Fully-grown Cloven sprout their own legs and arms and wiggle out of the patch to roam free, so these Cloven had to be mere children. They were small and pale with dark green spots on their bulbs.

Chasmira waved her hands frantically at the chattering cluster. "One at a time, please!"

"You want to go to the big city?" one of the tiny Cloven squeaked.

"Or the BIGGER city?" another whispered, and they all gasped.

"Oh dear," Chasmira said, clasping her hands. "Eh, I want to go to Argismora."

"Argie's Moors?" one of them mimicked, sounding confused.

"She said Argo's Moolah," said another, followed by more tittering laughter.

Chasmira groaned. "It's a city!"

The Cloven ooh'ed in astonishment. "Yes, we know about those!"

"You do?"

"We've never seen them, but we have heard all about it! Tall stone trees and many many people! Noisy things with wheels, all pulled by snorting four-legs with long hair! Going to the city!"

Chasmira clapped her hands, "Oh good, yes. When the snorting four-legs pulled the noisy wheeled things to the city, which way did they go?"

"That wayyy!" the Cloven all shouted in unison.

After a short silence, "Wait... which way?"

"That wayyy!" the Cloven all shouted in unison again.

The sorceress craned her neck, looking to the road. "North or south?"

"What's northorsouth?" the tiny mushrooms asked.

Chasmira looked up at Hakon with pleading eyes.

"I shall try," he sighed.

Hakon knelt down, his armored body casting a dark shadow over the tiny things. Before he could say more, the Cloven called up to him, "Hey, you don't have a mouth!"

"What? I hath a mouth," flustered.

"You have half a mouth?"

"Nay, a whole mouth!" more flustered.

"Where?"

"Under my armor!" most flusteredly.

"Can we have armor like yours?"

Chasmira rolled her eyes, "You know, if I didn't know any better, I'd swear you are a Cloven yourself under that imposing shell you wear. Confess now. It's all right, you're among friends."

The little mushrooms squealed with laughter.

Chasmira brushed off her dress as she stood up. "Alright then, look at me. The four-legged things walked upon this road. Tell me if the way I am walking is to Argismora."

"Argues Morning?" the Cloven puzzled.

"Oh you did say there were two cities, didn't you?" She fretted. "Hakon, is there a neighboring city larger than Argismora?"

"Nay," Hakon pondered, and then looked down to the Cloven. "I pray you, little ones, tell us from whence came the travelers through here? Camest they from afar?"

"The people on the wheeled things said they came from another place, a big city."

"And they were coming here, to a bigger city?"

The Cloven all thought for a moment before all shouting "Yes! They said the place they were going was bigger!"

"The highway from Holireath comes all the way north to Argismora! What other city could it be?"

Hakon nodded, "And Argismora would be the larger city?"

"I should know! I came all the way from home to find Magnate Argolvrecht here beyond the western mountains!" Chasmira clasped her hands together and rested them on her chin. "Now then, little ones! Did they walk this way to the bigger city?" and she began to walk in large, exaggerated strides.

The Cloven all laughed and exclaimed, "No, no, the other way!"

"Wonderful!" She turned on her heel, and waved for her towering companion. "Quickly, Hakon dear, we are going to Argismora! Thank you very much for your keen guidance, my little friends! Goodbye! Goodbye!"

~

They proceeded northward. After more than an hour of walking, the dark, gnarled forest was far behind. The two sorcerers now walked a dirt road that wound between rows and rows of lush green fir trees. Silvery morning light shone between the trees, sending bright beams across the road in a light mist that persisted in the air. The moist air felt warmer now that the sun reached through the firs.

"So, thy home is Holireath. It standeth to reason now," Hakon began.

"Whatever do you mean by that?" Chasmira answered, swinging her arms as she quickened her pace ahead of him.

"Why thou fled thy home. In peaceful Holireath, such power as yours is damnable."

Her arms lowered stiffly to either side.

"Thy parents dead, unable to send thee away. The White Aegis sorcerer also dead, unable to take thee away."

Chasmira's heart pounded. Her slender hands tightened in fists. "What of it, Hakon? What of it?"

Hakon hesitated. "Thou escheweth thy home now, yet thou lived there for many years. Thou didst live quietly, secretly... No one to ever discover you..."

"Yes. Yes, Hakon... no one ever discovered my sorcery," she snapped at his prying, whirling around to face him. "No one ever knew what happened or why I lived alone for so many years."

"Why didst you?"

"Why didst I what?"

"Live alone," solemnly.

"I wasn't like you, whisked away to the Phrontistery of First Fire when my power arose," she exploded at him. "Love changed to fear in my parents' eyes! I watched it happen. They would keep me in the house but not speak to me, as if I were vermin. Fear drove them to this, though I did not understand at the time. In my outrage, I confronted them about how estranged they were from me, and in my outrage, I summoned forth fire that destroyed them. Foolish child that I was... I see now only in hindsight that they were not afraid of me, but of what others might do to me.

"When the White Aegis sent their sorcerer from the sky, it was not to rescue me. It was to put me out of my misery. It was to find the fires of Chaos burning within me and snuff them out. But if my home was a castle and I the lone sentry, the infernal power within me was the moat. I summoned the beasts of the field to prey on my enemy and tear him to pieces. And none ever suspected a little girl," she coughed out laughter at the irony. "They suspected a dark sorcerer had killed my parents and then met an untimely end."

Hakon stood still as a pillar while Chasmira's words beat against him.

"So yes, I lived alone," her face taut as she chided him. "At home for as long as I could. The strange one, the bereft child, the orphan! I was pitied. Years passed before I searched for a higher purpose, for something greater than clinging to the memories left in my parents' humble little home."

Chasmira tore herself away from him, ashamed of her outburst. She did not know how she had let it all flood out, but there it was. It could not be unsaid now. Had she spent so many, many months staring wordlessly beside the Magnate's throne that it simply needed to burst forth?

"Therefore, didst thou leave. Thou left to become Magnate Argolvrecht's seer. But... why?"

The woman said nothing, but clasped her hands together and walked ahead of him.

"What awaitest thee in the Guardian City? Just another master to serve?"

She walked faster.

"Why not simply go back?" Hakon called after her.

"As I said to you earlier," shouting back at him, "I deny myself the vanity of fancying things that will never be... And I can never simply go back!"

No sooner had the words left her mouth then a blast of the purest searing white light erupted from the road ahead, throwing her backward to the ground! The forest shook with the force.

Chasmira sat up, eyes wide.

Two great wings spread from the tall, statuesque female figure now standing in the road. The feathers glistened like glass, as did the armor plates that clung to her body as if they were molded to her shape. Her shoulders were angular, her neck cranelike, her chin pointed. Her hair was as bright as a pearl. Her skin shone like clouds holding back the dawn. Her eyes glimmered like jade.

"Nandrzael..." Chasmira whispered.

Hakon froze, bathed in the white light. He knew this name: Nandrzael, a being of the realm above, an Angelic, and the patron guardian of Argismora.

"What.... happened, sorceress?" this woman demanded. Her voice echoed like the sound of war drums.

Chasmira stumbled and stood. Her knees were jelly, and she wobbled from foot to foot. "It all went as intended. Argolvrecht challenged the Mad Prince as you wished—"

"MIRIKININ IS DEAD, YOU FOOL!" the Angelic burst out, and the forest shook again. "They both are! I told you to lead Argolvrecht to the brink of war, not drive him over it headfirst!"

She was one of the mighty Angelics that oversaw the fate and future of lifekind. A visit from an Angelic was normally a blessed event. It portended a blessing once you completed a task for them. Though the tasks ranged from the grand to the mundane, a task from an Angelic usually set in motion a chain of events meant to accomplish good in the world. The end result could be hundreds of miles distant or many years away. Only the Angelics knew.

Almost unheard, Chasmira replied, "I merely—"

"You merely fed the idiot crumbs that would lead him to follow their trail, yes, a trail that led to the horde of the Mad Prince Mirikinin. Once provoked, the Prince would strike and Dimol Gol would be no more. The conquest of these lands would cease! Instead, both kings lie dead and all for nought!"

"It was his own rage that drove him over the brink, not I," the sorceress answered more firmly now. "What difference does it make? Are we not all the better now that we are rid of those beasts?"

"Those beasts, like all beasts, have whelps! The children of Mirikinin will hear of their father's demise. His blood calls to them out of the ground, and they will answer in time. They will shed the blood of thousands across these fair lands and all the country, and all because of you!"

Chasmira shuddered at the last three words. More blood on her hands.

"There is nothing now to be done. You have failed," Nandrzael pronounced in a grave voice.

"There is more yet to be done. You tasked me to move Argolvrecht to war and I did it. Give me the blessing."

The Angelic simply sneered. "You whispered to start a fire but did not shout to control it. Woman, your silence has made a madman into a martyr. There will be no blessing."

Chasmira clenched her fists at the last two words.

"Now there is only chaos," Nandrzael added.

"Argismora's lord may be swayed to seek Mirikinin's heirs and destroy them. The quest of an Angelic, or the prophecy of a sorceress—"

"Your theatrics have done enough."

"Please," forcing out the word.

Nandrzael looked pitilessly down at her. Her crystalline wings shifted shape slightly, and in a moment she was hovering ten feet off the ground.

"No. No, sorceress. Our bargain was life forfeited in exchange for life restored. A king and his kingdom, for a father and mother. Your chance for redemption has been squandered, and now it shall take at least a hundred years to undo what you have done this day. Fool that I was, I entrusted this to you... someone given to Chaos since childhood! All you do is leave death and destruction in your wake. I thought I could use it as a tool, but I see now this flame cannot be controlled."

Chasmira shut her eyes at the last word.

The Angelic continued, "It can only be snuffed out."

Chasmira's eyes snapped open in time to see a shower of bright white sparks! Nandrzael's shimmering sword, seemingly made of frozen vapor, wavered inches from her face... restrained only by Hakon's great iron staff parrying it!

Infernal flame swelled in Chasmira's eyes. "No. Like the others, you will BURN," unleashing streams of fire!

The gleaming Angelic moved like a blur to avoid the blast. A heartbeat later, Hakon swatted Nandrzael down with a twirl of his staff, leaving her facedown in the soil. He drove it downward between her shoulder blades, to impale her, but in a blur she was gone.

"Where did she go?" he growled.

Nandrzael's wings carried her with great speed and also silence, for Hakon did not notice as she appeared behind him.

"Hakon—" Chasmira screamed.

The sword pierced Hakon's armored shell like a stinger.

Black blood trickled out and then gushed as the Angelic yanked the vaporous blade back out of him. She watched Hakon's towering form topple over. "I'd pity you, dark creature, if I could."

A wave of fire engulfed her where she stood. Nandrzael shrieked in pain and spiraled up against a tree, before another stream of fiery hate struck her. It sent her spinning. The streams scorched straight through the tree trunk in seconds.

"BURRRNNNN! BURN, BURN, BURNNNN!!!" Chasmira howled.

When the fires died down, the forest fell quiet. Chasmira stepped carefully through the streams of silver sunlight. Her breathing shuddered as she looked this way and that.

She listened through the whispering crackles of flame on the tips of the tree branches. She listened hard for any gust of wind that might give away the Angelic's flight. Nandrzael was wounded, but the wound only made her angrier. Chasmira was useless to her. She would not spare her.

Moving shakily, the sorceress edged closer to Hakon's body. She forced her knees to bend and knelt next to him...

The Angelic struck like lightning, with a flash of brilliant light and the thunder of indignant rage! The force flung Chasmira backward off her feet. She landed against a fallen tree log. Nandrzael was right on top of her before she could even draw her next breath. She raised that blade of frozen vapor. The tip pressed against Chasmira's chest.

"Murderous scum," the gleaming Angelic spat on her with each word. The flesh of her face and neck were still sizzling, blotched black on one side, and her wing was wilted like a burnt flower. Her jade eyes glowed. "You have bereaved this world ten thousand lives today, for nothing!"

Chasmira's trembling lips curled into a smile. "Then what's one more?"

The forest echoed with a roar of primordial force, and Nandrzael shattered into bits, like a broken pot.

Strands of smoke rose from the prongs of the iron staff. Chasmira's white knuckles ached from how tightly she'd held it against the Angelic's ribs. She thought to drop it but instead raised it straight to brace herself, leaning her cheek against the cool metal.

Hakon. His body lay prostrate on the path. The massive suit of armor was now his coffin, and the forest his noble tomb. There was no way to move him or bury him now. "It is so strange to call someone friend, but what else can I call you? Thank you."

The ashes of the Angelic shimmered as the wind carried them away. Chasmira knew not if an Angelic could truly die. If not, it would take an army to repel the Angelic a second time.

An army...

Chasmira turned and walked off the path, through the fir trees. The sun was rising in the east before her, and she pushed through the light that increased with every step. Miles beyond the forest laid the jagged fields and deep grottos where Mirikinin's ironwolves were bred. It was only right that a firsthand witness brings the news of his death. By sundown the children of Mirikinin would meet a ragged sorceress with an iron staff and eyes of fire, summoning them to war. Perhaps she would get to pay a visit to the Guardian City of Argismora after all.

The view beside a throne was splendid indeed. This time, however, Chasmira would be the one sitting upon it.

SPIRIT OF THE WOOD

Adaline lunged over the next fallen tree trunk. Were they still behind her?

She swore she could hear the sound of the hoofbeats in the field she had just passed through. The ravine nearly lost her pursuers until one of them spotted her bright blue dress rising up the side of the hill.

Her steps pounded against the damp grass. Over the hill was a pockmarked glen. Beyond it was a minefield of spiny fungus bulbs. But beyond that, she saw a dense line of trees at the top of a steep hill!

The princess heard a hunting horn over her shoulder. She did not look back to see the charging mounts or Hector's hounds. All she focused on was the dense woods ahead.

She had made it this far.

She wasn't going home.

The steep, slippery hill would surely stop her pursuers. They would have to dismount to make the climb after her, and the foliage at the top looked thick enough to at least entangle them. The giant grazzurs the huntsmen rode were massive-shouldered boars, too large to fit through the trees... but were they strong enough to break through them if they somehow did scale the hill?

It was a chance worth taking.

Adaline grabbed fistfuls of long grass as she climbed up, as fast as she could. The moment she rose to where she could stand, she did not hesitate. She leapt toward the trees and into the shrubs...

She broke through the foliage, but her next step did not find solid ground.

She fell down the curved ravine that dropped so steeply right at the line of stabbing shrubs. Adaline rolled. The skirt of her dress caught on something and tore. She continued rolling and did not stop until she slid into the rain-steeped grass at the bottom.

~

Her knees and hands squished into the grass a little, and black mud bubbles came up where she touched the ground.

Adaline brushed aside her wet hair as she looked up to get her bearings. Before her stretched a deep and dense forest, filled with tall, pale, grey trees that reached skyward like long willowy arms before meeting the forest canopy. Overhead were leaves thick enough to blackout the sky almost entirely. Only here and there did the canopy allow thin strands of the daylight to pierce through like spiderwebs, down to the ground.

She walked a few hesitant steps forward, instinctively bringing both hands to fold over her chest. She had the feeling she was being watched.

Adaline's pale blue eyes looked from tree to tree, bush to bush. They finally fell upon a single plant sprouting from the midst of the wood, where red and gold leaves spiraled from its base like cobblestones in a street. She squinted at the plant's slender, wrinkled trunk and approached.

Her eyes followed the length of it up, up, up... and she began to back away.

The great creature was tall as an oak. Its body was shaped like a baluster. Its flesh looked like pleated linen but creaked like leather. Its head touched the top of the forest canopy, two red eyes peering down from the shadows. Some manner of a crown — perhaps antlers — were borne upon its head, for the leaves of the trees overhead rustled and shook whenever the creature moved.

Adaline staggered backward, but before she could run, a deep voice filled the air like a gust of wind.

"Do not be afraid. You are quite safe here."

The girl blinked and paused. "Who... who are you?"

A long, deep creak moved along the creature's body. "Why, I am Sythar, the spirit of the wood. Everyone around here knows my name."

Adaline shivered. The spirit of the wood's voice crooned with the deep hum of a loving mother's lullaby, but also gnashed like a snarling beast.

"Perhaps you do not know my name because you are not from around here," Sythar mused. "I pray you, tell me: where are you from?"

"From a land far away."

"Which land?"

Adaline stiffened. "What does it matter, spirit of the wood? I shall never return there."

"You shall not return if you remain lost in my woods," the towering spirit reasoned.

"I shall not return because I wish not to return."

The spirit stared down at her with the blood-red eyes of an owl. "And why is that?"

"Why? How could one return to a place where you are forced to do what your heart bids you not to... Where it does not matter what you feel, only that you do as you are asked. How could one return to a place where your love is taken away from you and given to another as if the unbetrothed were firewood, sold at market for a new pair of shoes?"

Sythar nodded his great horned head sympathetically. "It sounds like such disorder."

"But it is not disorder. It is order," now fuming, Adaline walked a circle around the towering spirit as if she paced around an oak. "It is cold, uncaring order. Like the stone of a mill, which flawlessly completes its task to grind, but will grind anything thrown into it."

"But not you. You have fled stones and found trees."

"Yes... Yes, I suppose I have."

Adaline cast a long look back toward the steep hill and the stabbing shrubs. She heard no din, no hunting horn, no hounds. She drew back a slow, shuddering breath and blew it out.

"What will you do now?" the towering spirit asked her.

"I don't know. I hadn't time to think of it. I simply knew that I needed to get away."

"So, what will you NOT do?" in a more intrigued tone.

"I will not be sold off to make alliance. I will not be betrothed to a whelp I have never even met! I will not belong to anyone! Just to myself."

Adaline began to walk idly. Long, wandering steps, winding between the grey trees. She ran her hands over each as she passed, swinging from them a little as she went.

"It was not always so. I did want to belong to one. He wished for it too, we both did! Not that it mattered. Some priss from over the mountains arrived with his daughter in a white carriage, white as a gourd. The priss had apparently come to give her in marriage... an agreement between their kingdoms. He and I met and he told me, see, in the field of daffodils and arrgodils that grew behind the coastline. We made a different agreement: to run off together on the morning of the wedding day."

The spirit of the wood nodded slowly, watching her from high above.

Her next step hesitated before continuing to wind through the long, pale trees, more slowly now. "It did not go according to the agreement. My father caught me returning home and kept me in my room all week. I laughed at the time because I know my beloved would have fled... and when I was free, I would leave and join him. At the first chance, I slipped out and ran. I came to the hiding place where we agreed to find each other. But he was not there."

Adaline stopped between the trees, her hands angrily gripping them tightly. "Whatever happened, it does not matter now. Either he was forced to go through with it, or forcing him was not necessary. But I did not find him this morning."

A deep creak echoed as Sythar turned away from her. "I feel such sorrow hearing of this. Such false hope, such heartbreak! It is no wonder you have come to find me."

"Oh I did not come to find you," Adaline replied before catching herself. Lest she sounds insulting to her host's company, she explained, "You see, I was found out at the hiding place and was then pursued by my father's huntsmen. I fled and fell down that very steep hill."

"Fear not, they shan't find you here," the spirit replied with slow, reaffirming words.

"No, they shan't."

"They do not dare. Child, I do not allow any malice to endanger the creatures that live in my wood. All is quiet and peaceful here."

Adaline smiled a little, forgetting the sadness of her tale. "It is peaceful. You must be quite powerful. No one hunts here?"

"No one."

"No one cuts lumber?"

"No one. My trees are sacred. Like cherished family to me... I could not bear to see one of them leave me."

"You have such a heart for things that cannot talk or walk," she mused as she began to walk between the pale trees again.

"Our hearts belong to many who once talked with us, walked with us, but cannot any longer. Many who are fond, who we would have kept if we could. The words and steps are fleeting in the moment, but eternal in memory."

Beyond the row of trees stood a large boulder, which Adaline climbed and then sat upon. From here she could see the expanse of the wood around her. To the south, east, and west, the wood stretched on and on in trails of pale, wiry trees. To the north rose the steep hill from whence she came, and Sythar standing before it, his red eyes still following her.

"Why do you watch me?"

"It has been a long time since anyone has come to walk in my wood."

"Well, you do not allow anyone to hunt or fell trees," she smiled at him through the gaps in the tree limbs between them. "My father has no interest in wooded places except for those things..."

Sythar's voice lightened. "That is a shame. My woods are beautiful. It is a shame that your father cannot appreciate simple, impractical things of beauty. To live under the shade, or lie in a bed of soft moss. To hold birds in your hands, and let rabbits sleep on your knees."

"I have never held a bird in my hands. But I have hoped and tried before!"

"The wrens and finches here would oblige you happily."

"Yes, that sounds wonderful!" Princess Adaline smiled wider. "Father would not enjoy the simplicity, but I would! Perhaps I should —"

"Not return home?" the spirit completed the thought. "No, you should not. Not to a place where you are sold and traded."

"Where shall I stay? In the wood?"

"Many have, before you set foot here yourself..."

The princess put a hand to her mouth to stifle a silent, breathless laugh. *To live here, in the wood!* Her teeth bit gently upon her lip, and she slipped her feet out of her shoes. The earth felt warm and soft from the recent rain. Tiny mushrooms bent beneath her step, and then puffed themselves back up when she lighted off them.

White flowers that hung like bells, in rows upon vines, brushed over her shoulders as she ducked and danced through them. She spread her arms high, and spun in place, teasing the ends of the willow trees...

Each tree lived in its own hiding place, and would always be there to meet you. The flowers would not betray but their sweet scent to anyone passing by. There was no order to it, and no orders to be given or obeyed. Perhaps the wood will be my new home. There was no hunting or woodcutting. You were simply one with the wood.

She continued to spin and dance through the long, pale trees, mimicking the way they bent by arching her back and reaching high like their long limbs. She laughed and curtsied to her partners, and walked over to shake hands in thanks for the lovely dance.

She froze and slowly drew back her hand, fingertips trembling. When she had touched the fork of the branches, it felt as if it were the contour of another hand she touched.

Her chest shuddered with each breath. *That couldn't be.* She backed away, and looked to another of the long, pale trees for comfort that it was just her imagination.

Instead, she caught sight of a gnarled lump above the crook of a limb. The lump jutted out abruptly and then sloped back where it joined the trunk, and had two holes on the underside...

Adaline, on reflex, reached up and touched her own nose.

A strange fright began to clamber from within her, gripping her throat from within. She wheezed and backed away, seeing now the knobbed elbows in the long, deformed white limbs that stretched skyward, begging for sunlight from the dark canopy above. In the winding feeder roots curled around the base of the tree, she saw legs curled as if sitting...

Her own legs crumpled beneath her as she slipped. Numbness had onset from the fright. But when she looked at her feet, her eyes grew wide with terror at the sight of tiny, puffy mushrooms that striped up her toes and had spread up to her anklebones. They tingled. They moved when she tried to wiggle her toes.

"What's wrong, child?" Sythar's voice echoed in her ears. Adaline threw herself back on her palms, staring up into the darkness.

A great wind welled up and tore through the wood! Great tree limbs shook, and flowered vines lashed like whips in its wake! A terrible creaking noise echoed through the air! Above the din, two red eyes flashed as the spirit of the wood leaned over her!

"Become one with the wood. Your great grinding stones are far away now! No woodsman shall ever lay you out for the mill, to be laid in pieces and sold. You are sacred to me," the spirit thundered in the gale.

"I don't want this!" the girl screamed in the wind.

"You lie as he lied! A hiding place you need never flee, never belonging to anyone! You will be cherished, and forgotten by all others!"

"My father —"

"He will never find this place, nor dare enter!" his voice now roared like a storm and yet shrieked like weeping widows. "I am the spirit of the wood! All who pass here tremble, for they know my name!"

"Let me go!"

"You wished for this! You wished not to return," he slavered.

No. Adaline clawed and crawled, every breath a wordless plea! Her knees dragged her numb feet across the leaves that spiraled across the wet ground. She grabbed fistfuls of warm, black mud that squirted between her fingers. Her knuckles ached with pain, but she ignored it in her terror.

The hill. The stabbing bushes. The only way out.

She did not dare look up. She was so near to Sythar she could feel his roots bulging in the ground beneath her, splitting the soil open. The creak of his movements were ear-splitting, even over the wind!

"Where are you going?" Sythar crooned sinisterly, a deep noise that made her bones shake. "Nothing awaits you there but punishment! The rod and the grindstone!"

"Father!" the girl screamed, clutching the mud and rock of the steep hill!

"His hunters are long gone, child! You are lost!"

Gristly soil jammed tightly under her fingernails. Her legs dragged uselessly behind her. Her eyes pinched shut against the wind and the mud that slid down on her...

~

The gloved hands gripped her arms so tightly, she cried out from the pain as she awoke. Adaline craned her bobbing head back to see Hector, her father's most trusted huntsman! Gently but hurriedly, he gathered her up into his arms and shielded her against the stabbing shrubs with his coat.

"She's alive, sire! Your daughter lives!"

As he turned and ran from the line of thick foliage, she saw Father hurrying to meet him. Hector traded the girl over to her father's arms, and together they secured her in the carriage.

Hector drove with great haste. "She was passed out at the steep of the hill. Must have exhausted herself trying to climb and lost consciousness!"

Adaline's head swam. The orange and red glens were a blur around her.

"After two days, I despaired of what oath more I could take before the heavens or the abyss," Father sobbed, "To see you return to me alive."

She wiggled her toes and began to weep. Father hugged her tightly.

"Adaline, my sweetest, my darling! Unto Hector I owe my debt forevermore, that he alone braved to enter the wood! It is the realm of a terrible creature of Chaos whose jealous power ensnares all trespassers, never to leave again. I feared you had fallen prey to this evil spirit... whose name I dare not speak, lest I invoke it out of thin air!"

She sobbed, "Sythar..."

THE HOBBLE

Logan A'Gally ran and rode

O'er hill and dale where it had snowed

Quick as a devil, fast as wind

As if something was after him

Nothing behind

Nothing in sight

Nothing to cause such fearful flight

But somewhere there lurked the Hobble.

His two friends, Branigan and Tuck

Never saw him so horror-struck

They dropped their fishing rods and ran

Over to lend a helping hand

He stuttered some

He stammered more

He stumbled off his horse and swore

"Gods save me I've seen the Hobble."

"What did you see? What did you hear?

A monster smiling ear to ear?

With eyes like moonlight when it's full?

A maw to easily eat you whole?

A bloodthirst roar

A fearsome cry

To freeze your blood right where you lie?

And yet you survived the Hobble?"

A'Gally paced and fumed and cursed

"The beast I saw was so much worse

It made no call, no fearsome cry

Nothing to warn when it's nearby

Just quiet steps

Just quiet breath

Just quiet creeping up like death

And just then you see the Hobble."

"Poor man!" they handed him a cup

And made a fire to warm him up

"The fish are shy, the day is spent

We've plenty of intoxicant

Brandy for cold

Rum for your nerves

We'll dine on bread and peach preserves

Forget all about the Hobble!"

Safe by the campfire, with his chums
Warm by the campfire, drinking rum
A rousing song to pass the night
A drunken dance to shake the fright
Loudly they laughed
Loudly they sang
Loudly they forgot sturm und drang
While silently watched the Hobble.

Oaths to Tyor, songs to Soth
Gods of duty and warlords wroth
Drinking to Naru, god of mirth
Drinking to anything on this earth
Later the night
Larger the fire
Lumber and drink thrown on the pyre
But such things attract the Hobble.

The moon enjoyed its promenade
O'er three men snoring where they laid
The fishers' rations strewn around
The empty bottles on the ground
The fire crackled
The white owl hoo'd
The hour might have been half past two
When Branigan heard the Hobble.

He grabbed a knife and looked around

He could have sworn he heard a sound

Of footsteps creeping in the snow

Just outside the campfire's glow

He stood up straight

He took a step

And Branigan, while his friends slept

Was gobbled up by the Hobble.

Mistaking moonlight for daybreak

Tuck was the next one to awake

He stretched and yawned and rubbed his eyes

He then fell backward in surprise

His friend was gone!

He stood up fast

He stopped and stared straight up, aghast

And staring back was the Hobble.

Two eyes like moonlight, bright and green

Shone down on the frightening scene

Rows of fangs in a smile so wide

Its mouth could fit a horse inside

Pale as a worm

Quiet as a mouse

Tall as a rich man's summer house

The roaming nightmare: the Hobble.

Yanked right out of peaceful dreams

By Branigan's and then Tuck's screams

A'Gally found a place to hide

A great oak log he crawled inside

He laid down still

He prayed for day

The one thing that could scare away

The deadly, ravenous Hobble.

But then he saw the strangest thing

He saw the Hobble shambling

Up to the campfire burning bright

And with all its murderous might

It crushed the pyre

It stamped and spit

It kicked up dirt to smother it

And darkness swallowed the Hobble.

In the Hobble's fit of fury

He saw his chance, he had to hurry

Silently but quickly acted

While the Hobble was distracted

A'Gally ran

Up hill and dale

And woke the village with a wail

"We all must beware the Hobble!"

"The Hobble makes no nest or den

Where do the Hobbles come from then?"

"Perhaps the dreams of sorcerers

My guess is just as good as yours

One thing is sure

Without a doubt

Always be sure your campfire's out

Or be gobbled by the Hobble!"

VOLGOTH JUSTICE

My fingers knotted themselves tensely as I stepped through the crowd. The women in our village square shouted "Thief! Thief!" and picked up stones to throw at the man knelt in our midst.

I shuddered as a voice rang over the din of the lynch mob like the sound of a church bell: "We shall have ORDER!"

His last word was followed by a hush that fell over the crowd faster than a single heartbeat. Even the black geese that fed near the fountain in our square, silenced themselves.

The Zealot Loesheron loomed over us all as he pushed his way through the crowd. He was tall and lithe, with shoulders broad as an ox's yoke. From his neck down he was wrapped in coal-black armored scales, overlaid with a longcoat of black bearskin. His skin was pale as the moon, and beneath his dark locks, his eyes were the dead green of a lizard's stare. I took a long, slow step backward as he slowly turned in a circle to survey the mob.

"What is the accusation? Speak, and there will be justice."

Alamech the Grocer stepped forward. "This man is a thief! He entered my store requesting a week's worth of supplies with no gold to pay for my wares! He tried to leave without paying!"

Loesheron's gaze fell to the man knelt on the ground. He was clearly a Jacorian... shirtless, with a pelt of brown foxtails for a belt and a long leather skirt. He was thickset, but I noted massive muscles beneath his hairy flesh with the strength of a well-fed war beast.

"That's not true," the Jacorian man growled back at his accuser.

No sooner had the words left his lips than Zealot Loesheron took a single lunging step toward him, catching the large man's jawline with the back of his hand.

"Speak with care, barbarian, how you accuse a citizen of Volgoth!" the Zealot hissed. "A liar is worse than a thief."

"I am no thief," the Jacorian replied, reeling from the blow as his mouth bled. "I had gold in my pouch when I arrived at the shop. Before I could pay, a thief in a cloak took the pouch off my belt. I left the shop in pursuit. It was my error that I was holding the food."

"There was no thief in my store," the grocer said.

"Thieves make a point not to be seen by grocers, I believe."

"Judge Loesheron, he makes light of his crime!"

The villagers around me began to shout with Alamech for the man to be whipped or stoned. To be publicly beaten was the least punishment available for a thief in Volgoth. I anxiously ground my teeth, watching the burly man sweat.

"I was robbed, I tell you!" he shouted.

Loesheron approached him like a snake, coolly kneeling to look him in the eye. "You claim a thief stole your gold, and yet you have no proof of the thief, or that you even had any gold to begin with. I must heed the word of the people, for their judgment is law unto us all."

"Your people hunger for judgment on me like swine hunger: they'll take the first thing set before them."

Loesheron bared his teeth in a scowl and put his hand to the sword on his hip. "Confession is done in the dark. Every guilty whisper is heard in a crowd. Your doubt is guilt enough for me, you pathetic bleating ewe."

With that, he stood and shrugged. "Stone him outside the village and leave him for the fowl."

The man could not get to his feet soon enough before the crowd seized his limbs, binding his hands behind his back. He roared in protest while Loesheron turned his back, his black fur coat swaying with the weight of the armored rings woven into it.

"No justice," the Jacorian bellowed after him, "Where a man may buy the judge's dinner with the blood of the innocent, and he'd never know!"

I saw Loesheron's face slowly clench from stinging conviction, and he turned and lifted a hand. The crowd froze mid-step with their prisoner.

"Let it not be said that the Zealot of Cannirath would not search his own house for a traitor. You say the thief was a man?"

"Aye," the Jacorian panted. "A young man, not a day past twenty winters."

The Zealot made a broad sweeping motion toward the crowd around them. "Then let every man younger than twenty years old, come forward! We will let the eyes of the accused betray the true thief if he exists."

We assembled: eleven of us including myself, being barely fifteen years old. The onlookers jeered at the large northman as he carefully looked over each of us.

"He's stalling! Let the birds have him!" they cried out.

Finally, the Jacorian's grey eyes set upon me. I returned his gaze.

"That one... he's the one who took my pouch."

The crowd erupted with confusion and fury. Zealot Loesheron lifted his finger to his lips and began to walk toward me thoughtfully, preparing to question me. I began to shiver.

"No!" a man shouted above the crowd, stepping forward in my defense. It was my father: fifty years old, streaks of grey in his hair, and leaning upon a crooked ravenwood cane to support his weak leg. He fumed and jabbed a finger toward the Jacorian without looking at him.

"Good Judge, he mocks the justice of our kingdom and of our lord the Ever-King! Your just wrath should not be so easily turned when this man condemns his own jury! My son could not have stolen the gold, he was beside me all morning from dawn till this very minute!"

I held my breath as the crowd was quiet and the judge still. Then, like the first cricket at dusk:

"That is not so," a woman in the crowd stated.

I shivered again.

"You stood and fed the geese at the fountain at sunrise, and this you did alone for over an hour," she said. "See now, where your basket of bread still sits by the fountain!"

Zealot Loesheron looked to the fountain, seeing that indeed Father's basket still sat where he did before I was called into question. The tall judge strode past the woman and through the crowd, which parted for him like grass parts for a gale wind. Lifting the basket gently, he returned with it to stand between my father and the Jacorian man, who at this moment gaped at us with utter disbelief.

"I would hope that your geese lay golden eggs for you," Loesheron said, and he dropped the basket. The leather pouch under the napkin spilled Jacorian gold across the stone at his feet.

"Every guilty whisper is heard in a crowd," the judge repeated. His green eyes met mine and narrowed with indignation as his fingers closed around the hilt of his sword.

I felt a warm rush from my heart to my throat, and my ears rang hard for a few moments. My eyes had followed the swing of Loesheron's longsword, its dark steel now slicked with blood. It was with incredible difficulty that I drew in a labored breath and fell to my knees.

The Zealot's back was to me. From behind his towering silhouette, I saw Father's headless body topple onto the street.

"Grocer, give this barbarian his gold and the food he needs and send him away. He has done no wrong."

"What of the body?" the woman asked.

"Let the fowl have it."

"What of the lad?"

"A liar is worse than a thief. I will not punish him."

The crowd nodded with approval, and removed Father's body from the square, complimenting the judge's fairness between themselves with excitement. A chilling wind from the mountains began to pick up strength, ringing the chimes that swung from the porches of every house in the village.

The burly Jacorian, freed from his bonds, swept his gold off the ashen street and stepped to Zealot Loesheron's side. His look was a mixture of disbelief and gratitude.

"I don't understand... why kill a liar but not punish the thief too?"

The Zealot answered with an impassive reptilian stare over his black fur collar. "A thief can pay back that which has been stolen. The truth cannot be repaid by a liar. Coins can be counted, but lies are endless."

I bent down, picked up the basket, and walked over to the woman, still standing in the square where the other villagers had left. She offered me a soft smile and her small, calloused hand. I took my mother's hand and we returned home.

THE WITCH HUNTER

T was the eighth day of Luthiam, Month of Rains, when I rode into the Silvanian town of Mondkirk. Brightly colored windmills greeted me on the hilltops as I traversed the winding roads that swelled and fell like waves. In all directions, I saw no trees, only tall spring grass. Orange wildflowers grew in clusters that peeked between the knee-high stalks.

The scenery was a pleasant diversion from the task at hand. I didn't ride a hundred and sixty miles to admire wildflowers.

The Silvanian town lay twenty-one miles south of the wealthy port city of Navale. The inhabitants of Mondkirk were no less affluent. The pompous aristocrats spent their time hunting, riding, fencing, dancing, vapor-bathing, courting... and no doubt gulping down sweet, red queensapple brandy to accompany all the aforementioned sport. Silvanians enjoy most of their daily activities with a glass of liquor in their bellies. As you well know, the "Silvanian swagger" they boast to have from birth, would be more aptly called the "Silvanian stagger."

I espied such a stagger from a young man outside the fenced yard of a sizable manor. He leaned back against the brass gate, elbows on the bars. Not much older than sixteen he was, his hairless chest bared out of an unlaced white shirt.

"You've missed the party, white knight." He grinned up at me, eyes half-focused in the morning light. With a toss of his head, he moved one of his dark, curly locks out of his eyes.

"The party hasn't started yet."

The lad's brows furrowed. "Whaddya mean?" Noisy brat.

"Whose house is this?"

"Eh?"

More slowly, "I say, who is the master of this fine, respectable house?"

"Ahh, that'd be my uncle, the Viscount al'Ranta."

"Thanks," I replied. The grin fell from the lad's face as my horse kicked open the gate, and I rode toward the house with great speed. I heard him shouting and cursing in the dust behind me.

It so happened that the Viscount al'Ranta was outside the manor house, watching one of his servant girls chop wood. His looks were similar to the staggering brat at the gate, but with grey in his hair and a sagging pot belly under his tunic. The viscount stood with one foot up on the woodpile, puffing his pipe and admiring the slender lass as she worked. The thunder of my horse disturbed his morning rumination.

"What's this? You'd better have a damn good reason to come storming across my land uninvited," he snarled at me.

"My apologies, Your Grace, but I have business in town and I like to come into a place well-informed. You seem a man with many acquaintances, so I shall begin with you." and I started to let myself down off my horse.

The viscount seemed to be in an inhospitable spirit, for he grabbed the axe out of the servant girl's hand. "I told you, you are unwelcome on my land."

"Uninvited, not unwelcome," with a hearty laugh. "I solicit such an invitation now, from the lord of the manor, if he be so kind."

"You'd find such a thing in a sealed note and handwritten with my quill."

I perceived the smell of salvia from his pipe.

"I've no patience for pompous Alcimaeans who think they can trample my land, witlessly crusading in the name of their ancient kings!" he drooled with slurred words, hefting the axe and swinging it for my ribs!

His choice of herb impaired him badly, for the axe blade merely bounced against the white steel of my plate armor. I never am without it, you see, even while sleeping. Especially while sleeping.

The dim viscount shivered from his own blow, stumbled, and would have fallen had I not seized him by the shirt and lifted him into the air. I drew his face close to the vents of my helmet.

"You are quite mistaken then, Your Grace, for I come not in any name but my own... Bacchus, son of Jeovan. I come here to seek and burn a witch, and I shall need but a few minutes of your time to help me with this little errand. Now, shall we go inside, and I'll find you your quill?"

~

A Chaos sorcerer will be feared and despised, but a blood-witch is not suffered to live in these lands. I do not mean that they are easy to destroy by any means...

Their practice is an abomination among sorcerers. The Arts of True Sorcery enable one to draw from the primordial powers: Odic sorcery from the heavens, Divine from life itself, Macabre from death, Feeric from the scales of luck, and Elder from order. I myself am proficient in both Divine and Elder sorcery... only valuable things those old fools in the White Aegis taught me after taking me from my widowed mother many moons ago.

Blood witchcraft, on the other hand, draws power from a dark, forbidden source: the blood goddess of Avgannon: realm of the dead. In ancient texts of the Mazigoric covens, her name is literally translated as "The Crone." More liberal translations of the text call her "the ancient mother," for in their legends she is the Mother of Titans... the first being ever created by the Makergods eons ago when this world was a world entirely different. The Titans nearly destroyed that world, fighting each other for domination.

In the writings of the great hero Androxes, he saw the Crone with his own eyes, describing her as "a well of eternal life, trapped in the chains of eternal undeath." She is a prisoner goddess, forever bound in the realm below to create, but never to rule. Thus is she chained, and in like manner she chains all who serve her — to receive her power is to receive her curse. Her offspring now are mostly warriors for the death god of Avgannon. Those unfit for his service are cast out to die or wander, so misshapen that they are confused for the creatures of Chaos. I could not possibly tell you which are deadlier.

All the Crone ever wanted was for her children to be great.... what, I suppose, any mother would want. Blood witchcraft tempts those who desire greatness or vengeance. Those who swear by her name, call her mother, and learn the cursed tongue of the Mazigorn, must forever be faithful. She gifts blood-witches with great power, and burdens them to obey her dark whispers. In their obedience, however, they must shed blood to appease her.

The witch I now pursued menaced the free lands between Alcimaea and Silvany. I serve neither crown. I simply cannot see this abomination continue to soak the land in blood. My kin in Alcimaea, good people that they are, make play at diplomacy when they should be drawing swords. If they had, two villages and an entire grudge of Ogres would still be alive.

Fools.

The viscount was exceptionally helpful after our sobering exchange in the yard. The manor was a hub of gossip, and I quickly gained an intimate familiarity with Mondkirk's residents.

The witch would not pass up the opportunity to prey upon the vulnerable aristocracy. She had fled only a few hours ahead of me, and had not rested the entire day before. Without a doubt I suspected she came here for shelter until nightfall. The viscount's neighbors across the orchard field and past the distillery were away on a hunting trip. Their manor was unoccupied, and a perfect place for a vagrant witch to hide.

Bidding my reluctant host a fond farewell, I set off across the amber field. The morning sun had vanished into clouds that presaged rain later. I felt disappointed, until I remembered the viscount's firewood was stowed in a shed and would be quite dry.

Not even fifty yards from the house, I noticed beside me walked a young man — the very same junior al'Ranta from earlier at the gate.

"So you are a witch hunter," squinting up at me.

"I am one today."

"Do the knights of the ol' golden kingdom normally hunt witches?"

"The knights of Alcimaea are honor-bound to pursue whatever and whoever they are tasked to seek, to the ends of the world. It is a great shame upon a knight to return empty-handed. There are some who have never returned from their tasks yet, whose lives are dedicated to their completion."

"Truly?" he blinked in disbelief.

"Aye, truly."

"And thus are you bound?"

I sighed, "Something like that."

"What place insists on your presence next?"

"That humble longhouse at the end of the field."

There was silence for a few steps.

"I'll come with you, Bacchus, son of Jeovan," the youth spouted.

"What for? Did you leave your flask over there?"

"Don't be vulgar. I keep a spare on me at all times."

"Is it enough to share?"

"You wish."

I laughed loudly at the lad's stubbornness. "Indeed! Depending on what we uncover there, you may need every drop of fortitude yourself."

Crossing the rest of the field, we arrived at the neighbors' longhouse. It was a broad one-story home made of handsome grey stone and accented with dark hardwood trim — like a country home a royal family would summer in. Around the yard was a split rail fence my horse could not jump, so I looped his bridle around a post and ducked between the rails.

The house showed no sign of forced entry, but of course, that meant nothing. Locks could be picked and latches broken.

"Do you seriously think there's a witch hiding here?"

I rolled my eyes back so far I thought I might knock my helmet off. "What's your name, lad?"

"Ethan. Ethan al'Ranta..."

"Thank you, Ethan. I shall remember your name, so that when the witch steals your voice and puts it in a bottle, I will be able to introduce you to young ladies who want to express their pity."

Ethan fell silent so quickly, I almost stopped my survey of the house to make sure he was not already bewitched.

Scanning around the whole house fully, I determined that entering through the front or side doors was foolish. Anyone inside could easily be waiting to ambush me the instant I entered. I considered burning the house down as an alternative.

No. The neighbors wouldn't like that.

Given the Silvanians' fondness for drinking, I set about to find a door that may lead down into a wine cellar, and I found it shortly.

I drew my shield to batter my way in. One broken cellar door later, I was searching between giant wine barrels that stood on either side of the lower level. It was cool and moist down there, and my footsteps were very soft as I treaded the stone floor.

I whispered an enchantment quietly under my helmet. *"Immach Scatthan Asber..."*

Beyond my normal five senses, a sixth stirred awake to search for the life energies of any living thing around me. Slowly I crept along. I kept my hand on my sword hilt. Mice, I sensed. Crickets. I crept further, looking between the wine barrels. Spiders and more rodents. Wood lice. My perception reached out into the far recesses of the cellar.

From above in the house, I heard something clatter and echo. I stood taller, looking up and stretching out with my feelings. My sword slipped silently from its sheath as I made my way toward the stairs up into the house. Total explosive surprise was my only option, for a witch forewarned of an attack is deadly.

I glanced back only momentarily to check on Ethan. He was squatted, his eyes wide with fear, on the stairs where I had entered. I waved to him to wait. I crouched on the stairwell up into the longhouse, and at that precise moment she stepped within range of my sixth sense.

A small calico cat, that is.

She was padding across the floor toward the door, probably smelling me. It had been a few days since my last proper bath. I cleared my throat and whispered under the door to her in the Elder tongue. *"Bruid an Bheith..."* I then followed with, "Hello there."

The cat meowed in reply, but the enchantment I had cast allowed me to hear, "You are trapped in the cellar? Fool."

"Not trapped. Searching for something," I replied. "Prithee, is anyone else at home?"

"No, my two-legged pets left a few nights ago. I let them go out now and then to play and stretch their legs. Last year one of them came back ready to have kittens of her own! She only had one, though..."

"And no other visitors recently?" I asked.

"Nothing but a few mice I killed. I've got one left if you want me to fetch one and bring it to you?" she offered.

"No thank you, I'm trying to cut down," abruptly ending my interview with the feline. I strained with my sixth sense. I listened for any other stir besides this lone housecat. Nothing.

I cursed to myself.

"She isn't here," growling to Ethan. I stormed out of the cellar and back into the yard.

Where could she have gone? There is no way she would leave herself exposed in such a populated place. Sleeping under a bridge, or under the shade of a river willow would attract attention. Silvanians were exceedingly territorial and nosy. A fisherman, a boatman, or a rider would happen upon her and interrogate her thoroughly.

My eyes scanned the countryside. The other manors were occupied. She would have to murder her way inside one of them. Was the witch that desperate? I came to stop a massacre, not mop the blood from the floor.

"She isn't here?" Ethan parroted as he walked to my side.

Wind rippled across the lumpy green grass of the yard. Thunder rumbled in the distance as I answered, "No, she is not. And so our search begins anew."

Ducking back through the fence rails, I untied my horse and began walking across the field to the main road through Mondkirk. As I walked through the golden knee-high grass, however, I thought better of my retreat.

"Ethan, we passed a distillery on the way here, did we not?"

"We did, yes."

"What say we stop by and re-fill that flask of yours?"

Shortly, we reached the distillery. It was two stories tall, with slanted tile roofs, stone pillars, and walls of wattle and clay. The crooked little building was quaint. We sauntered up to the front door curiously.

It pays to be cautious. With but a look over the door, I held out my arm to bar Ethan from opening it.

"Heed me, lad. Do not touch the door with your hand."

I pointed to a dark red stain on the door about the size of a man's palm. It was an irregular pentagon shape with red lines radiating out all around it. Within this shape was a circle, with a dot in its center.

"What is that?"

"That symbol you see stained into the wood is the cursed Sign of Hilif. Whosoever touches an object bearing it, receives the sign in their flesh and the curse along with it. Were you to receive it, I would have to fight myself not to rend you in pieces with my bare hands. The curse evokes intense malice from anyone who beholds you."

I drew the shield from my back, pushed the door open with it, and then laid it down to brace the door open behind me.

Not a moment too soon. Rain started drizzling down, dripping off the tiled overhang. I was right about those clouds. As much as I did not want to leave the lad to soak outside, it was too dangerous for him to face the witch at my side.

"Stay behind with my horse, Ethan. The last thing we need is to be baited into leaving this witch a ride out of here," I said, and I left him in the rain.

Inside, the distillery stunk of coal and the smell of burnt almond — a byproduct of too much direct heat under the stills of liquid. Typical of the Silvanians to rush the refining process in their greed. Directly ahead was a flight of wooden stairs leading to the second floor. To the left and right were identical doorless rooms containing tall metal cylinders with pipes that reached upward through the ceiling into the second story.

I noticed a spiderweb gleam in the stream of light from the door, and espied the arachnid in its web. Leaning in close, I muttered the enchantment "*Bruid an Bheith*" and whispered, "Prithee, is anyone else staying here?"

"Aye," said the spider in a tiny voice like the creak of a cupboard. "My sister upstairs and her forty-four children..."

"I'll tell her you said hello, but are there any humans or otherwise you haven't seen before?"

"Aye, that dark creature upstairs. Slipped in here like one of my own kin and made herself at home."

"At last. Thank you," hungry for the hunt. "Your web is lovely, by the way."

I thought to draw my sword, but my heavy footsteps on the old wood stairs were already concern enough to me. I clung to the wall as I ascended, easing my armor-encased mass along.

My eyes strained to see. As I reached the top of the flight, a flash of lightning illuminated the loft. I could see the shine of the metal alembic into which the pipes from downstairs fed. The distilled spirits would collect here, purified, and ready to be poured out. The metal drums were perfect places to hide. I would have summoned my sixth sense to search, but I durst not speak lest I give myself away.

Thunder rumbled through the distillery. The alembic and the rafters rattled, and the plates of my armor rang against each other. Quickly, I braced myself against a timber at the top of the stairs, hoping I could stop the vibration. The thunder continued to roll. The distillery pipes let out a whine where they touched the floorboards.

My teeth were grit tightly as the thunder trailed off. I waited. All I heard was the rain against the tile, plinking like the sound of a spoon tapped against a bowl. I let out a breath and took the last step up into the loft.

There was a crackle behind me, and the echoing roar of pure rage.

The next thing I knew, I was midair, falling along with the raindrops and a thousand bits of the shattered wall. I stared up into the clouds and flipped over as I fell, looking down into the grass as I landed flat.

I groaned. I felt like I'd been kicked by a horse. Rainwater, pooling in the field, drained out of my helmet's faceplate as I put my palms down and lifted myself up.

The rain pattered loudly against my armor. I stood and centered myself, squinting up at the distillery through the rain. Half of the second story had been ripped open. Bits of broken timber hung from the gaping hole that opened with the force of the blast. This blood-witch was strong indeed.

I chuckled and drew my longsword. My hundred-and-sixty-mile ride was not for nothing.

"Bacchus!" I heard Ethan's shouting faintly behind me as he tried to control my horse. While keeping my eyes fixed upon the building, I reached my right hand back toward the lad.

"Ethan, *Tuhhus-walh*!" casting an enchantment of the divine on him. Lattices of pure radiance wrapped around his torso and limbs, creating glowing bands of armor. I could not allow him to be harmed in the impending battle.

"Steady your nerves, lad. She'll feast upon your fear to gain strength."

I heard the groan of metal from the front door, and I saw the shine of my shield borne up in someone's grasp. It proceeded forward out of the doorway, into the rain. The figure carrying it was dark as shadow, shrouded in long, tattered cloth like a widow in mourning. Only her bare feet showed themselves as she trod through the tall grass toward me.

Halfway between me and the distillery, she lifted a hand, turning it to extend her forefinger and middle finger together while pointing the other two fingers down together.

The sign of destruction. The Death God's sign.

"*Me Ur Hūdăk*!" I shouted, funneling divine might into my sword.

Even as I did, a crackling orb of pure rage formed at her fingertips. She raised it over her head, and hurled it! It tore through the air with the roar of a gale storm! There would be no truer test of our skills. The first time in the loft I did not see it coming. This time I challenged her power with my own. I charged forward, driving my sword up and into the orb!

The flash was brighter than lightning! The orb arced away high over my head, landing in the crown of a queensapple tree at the back end of the field, blowing it to pieces.

I laughed, spreading my arms to the shrouded figure. "I'm impressed. I have deflected a volley of arrows with a single swipe of my sword using that enchantment. I am untouchable," returning the blade to a low guard position, "Even against the likes of you."

I charged through the rain at her. I dropped two thunderous blows, but she slunk under them using my shield as protection. She moved with a crouched gait like a vulture. Her dark veils made her appear as little more than a shadow beneath the shield. I spun to follow her, whipping my cape behind me to keep it clear.

In a foolish move, I raised my sword to shoulder height to stab down at her. When I did, she leapt inside of my strike and jammed my shield between my shoulder pauldron and my chestplate, which forced my hands apart!

Her hand touched my throat. I heard a croak of forbidden words in that abominable language. I grabbed for her and she recoiled, but when I tried to speak my next enchantment no sound would rise out of my throat. The witch! She had stolen my voice!

I panicked. Without summoning my sorcery I had no chance of stopping her. I harnessed the panic into swiftness and charged, swinging to catch her in the head or neck with the butt of the sword hilt.

Alas, the witch was too quick. She ducked and dodged my attacks, leaving me no other choice.

I dropped to one knee in a lunging strike, driving my longsword through her veils and into her ribs. As I did I heard her whisper again. I knew what would come next.

The pain in my ribs hit harder than I anticipated, and I nearly fell to my side. Had I fallen, it would have meant death. Instead, I pushed off with my bent leg and knocked her backward, spearing her to the ground! As I did I felt the flesh break open in my back, and blood ran fast under my armor.
I had a minute, no more. With one hand I held the sword tightly. With the other, I tore at her veils, desperately searching. It had to be on her somewhere!

At last, I heard the jangle of porcelain. My gauntleted hand jostled a necklace with finger-sized porcelain vials strung on it! I pulled it free with a firm yank and raised my hand to smash the vials on the ground.

Before I could, I heard a crackling hiss and saw a bright flare of power.

I tumbled end over end, skimming the tall grass but not hitting the ground for about sixty feet. I landed face-down on my hands and knees, skidding to a stop. My chest ached to breathe. My hands tingled like they were numb limbs. I mouthed a curse, still voiceless.

Before me, the witch rose to her feet and started toward me. Lightning flashed behind her. I had only moments left to reflect. She was much more powerful than I anticipated to overcome me with such a rudimentary hex. Nevertheless... Bacchus, son of Jeovan, has never fled against a child of the Crone in his life. I pulled myself up and stood, still bleeding but still clutching my longsword with a granite grip. It was all I had left.

Just then, I noticed Ethan behind her, crawling on his hands and knees through the stalks. Then, he sat up with the necklace of vials in his muddy hands. He looked at me with wide eyes. His hands shook. I heard the crackle between the witch's fingers...

Ethan drew the metal flask from his pocket, and smashed the vials to bits against it!

"*PARÁ HANDANDÁTAR!*" I roared!

My voice echoed through the valley, and from my body erupted a burst of light! The stalks of grass glowed like sun rays and the raindrops shone like stars for a single instant.

To anyone within three hundred feet of us, the world had gone white with searing light. The witch's scream was unearthly as she clutched at her eyes, tearing at her own rain-soaked veils.

It was as if she was staring into the sun. I simply watched her thrash about in agony while I selected my next enchantment.

"*Ziladuwa Arha Dā-ēshar*," I growled.

I felt my wound knit in seconds. Fresh blood flowed in my veins as if never spilt. I gripped the sword with renewed strength.

Meanwhile, that dark creature shook off the blindness. A long tear in her veil permitted me to see part of her face: black veins streaked across her skin, and a bright blood-red eye stared back at me.

Lightning flashed overhead. Thunder pounded loudly.

The witch turned toward Ethan, and began to utter some abominable pronouncement. However, I refused to let her have her say.

"*Srian Fein*!" I interrupted, reaching forth with my hand toward her.

The witch arched backward as if clutched in the grip of a monstrous, crushing claw. My enchantment of rebuke held her firmly, fight though she did. My will was made of steel stronger than my armor. I raised my hand, carrying her high into the sky. I would let the storm have her.

She screamed a final cry of rage before a bright bolt of lightning tore straight through her! Her veils ignited in a burst of red flame!

Ethan ran to my side, soaked and utterly breathless. "Do… Do you think she's dead?"

I dropped my hand down. Her veils fluttered as she fell to the ground with a loud crunch.

"Yes lad," I replied. "I do believe she is."

~

Not long after, I returned to the Viscount al'Ranta, who— as you might imagine — was very happy hearing about my successful hunt and even more so hearing about my imminent departure. I asked him for some firewood for the witch's pyre, and he told me that I could have any I was willing to chop myself. I did so with his slender servant girl keeping me honest, one foot up on the woodpile as she watched me work.

I burnt the witch's remains, to ensure that her body is never found and resurrected by the Crone's children. Thus did I to purify the land in the name of all that is merciful and good.

"My work here is done. I bid you farewell, young Ethan al'Ranta," I said as I settled myself atop my horse. "It turned out that you would save me, and not the other way around as I presumed. You are full of surprises."

"The kindest surprise would be to see you again, Bacchus, son of Jeovan."

"Wish not for such a thing, for the only reason to return over these borders would be for another hunt and another pyre."

Ethan smirked, tossed his curly locks, and raised his flask into the air. "Then I toast to your continued success, and that we never see each other again."

As I sped away on my horse across the hills of spring grass and between the colorful windmills, I mused to myself. Silvanians. To them, even a witch hunt is a sport, celebrated with toasts and brandy, but to me, it is a sacred duty I must fulfill. Young Ethan assumed me to be returning to the white castles of Alcimaea, but my next venture called me westward... to frozen, savage lands every bit as unforgiving as the beasts who rule them.

But that is a tale for another time.

THE DUEL

I t was calm and cool that day in the wood. It was mid-Flannared, the autumn colors had turned, and the sun was that much more brilliant through the golden leaves over the white birches. The red barongrass stood three feet high, which provided excellent camouflage for creatures hiding from any predators.

The creature in this case was a certain thief, who had made his way out of the borders of civilized lands, and made camp here in the glades of the wood. The scent of smoking lamb over hot coals was an indulgent risk taken after a two-day journey into no man's land.

Crouched behind him and enjoying the cover of the barongrass, was a certain Alcimaean knight clad in silver and red. Tracking him all the way from the hunting hamlets of the borderlands, he'd spent two days on his trail. It is a small wonder that the scent of lamb would gain his attention.

The thief was wanted in Alcimaea, Volgoth, and two provinces of Jacore for six counts of highway robbery and beast theft. More importantly, the manhunters hired to pursue him previously had wreaked fourfold the havoc of his original crimes that demanded their hire. This had to end.

Therefore was Phoelius sent: a cunning knight of Alcimaea's west quarter, carrying the crest of the white bear on his shield. Handpicked by Tetrarch Hadrean for the task, Phoelius was renowned for being patient, resourceful, and savvy in battle.

Phoelius secured the man's hands behind his back with rope, and then searched him. No potions, poisons, or weapons. Satisfied, he took hold of the rope's end and started the long walk back to Ellishelm.

The steward of Ellishelm was a just man, and fair. In Alcimaea, a thief was always sentenced to repay double the value of the stolen goods. Given this man's poor state, it was unlikely that the thief would be able to repay. A creditor would have to pay it for him, and the thief would be sentenced to work to repay the debt in bondage. Given the modesty of the town, the steward would likely name himself creditor and decide the thief's sentence. Given his mercy, the sentence would likely be short.

The pair walked for a good stretch through the tall red grass and between the papery tree trunks. Yellow leaves drifted down like falling snowflakes.

The dark figure stood out immediately in the sunny glade.

Phoelius thought to simply keep walking, but he knew that would be impossible. He paused, keeping his breath even while he looped the rope around the trunk of the closest tree. The figure — armor and cloak both black as night, topped with a head of thick dark hair — started toward them.

It only stopped when Phoelius' shortsword drew with a bright ring.

"That's far enough, thank you," he called out.

Pale green eyes peered out from under the dark locks. A chill went through Phoelius, and his jaws tightened.

A Volgothan.

"I am Loesheron... the Zealot of Cannirath."

Black armor scales flexed and bristled like a lizard's spikes along his whole body, and his cloak trailed behind him like smoke. He circled halfway around them, counterclockwise. It was as if he were testing to see if his mere presence would send the Alcimaean into retreat — a worthy first tactic, for to say his presence was intimidating would be an understatement. Phoelius was not short by any means, yet the Zealot stood a full head taller than him. His reach would be longer too, Phoelius instinctively calculated.

"This man has committed crimes against Volgoth, against our lord the Ever-King. I will take him for judgment."

"This man is a citizen of Alcimaea and will return back into our borders under my charge," Phoelius affirmed.

"By what law do you claim him, knight?"

"By the law of my land—"

"But we are not IN your land! We are in no man's land... How pitiful are the laws of your kingdom to be barred by borders and lines on a map—"

"By what law do YOU claim him, then?"

"By the law of my word, Alcimaean! I am Volgoth! I am decreed to bring the rule of my law with me, wherever I go and whithersoever I speak!"

"Then hold your tongue, and I shall let you keep your head."

"Threats?"

"I stand here before you with sword drawn, and it is my words that threaten you most?" the knight smirked and clicked his tongue. "Fragile creature."

Zealot Loesheron's green eyes narrowed into slits, and his gloved fingers curled around his sword hilt. The longsword's fine steel was the color of storm cloud, and it resonated with a ringing that lingered in the air long after it was drawn.

"I shall afford you your free will. Leave, or fight."

Phoelius smiled. "No man affords me what is already mine."

"Your tongue will be the first thing I cut out."

The first strike lashed at Phoelius in a blur of dark steel. A sharp whining noise echoed through the air as the longsword sliced it. The second strike came just as fast. Phoelius raised his shield! The clamor of metal sent birds scattering out of their hiding places for hundreds of feet around.

The next strike severed a low limb clean off the white birch. Before Phoelius could counterstrike, he ducked one more that hit the trunk. The sword continued straight through! The tree buckled and fell with a crash into the waist-deep red grass.

His foe was not a duelist, but an executioner. Each swipe of the Zealot's sword was meant to cleave him in two, or take off his head. Each swipe also took full advantage of the longsword's reach and its wielder's long limbs.

The Zealot's fighting style was explosive. Strides forward were long and aggressive. Backsteps were short and few. His longsword, glimmering with the dark rage of a storm, held a razor's edge.

Phoelius growled. This fight could be one-sided no longer. This son of Volgoth must be shown he is playing in a lion's den.

He raised his shield against the Zealot's next blow, and followed with a shield rush to force his enemy back! As soon as the shield collided with the Zealot's body, Phoelius felt dirt mound up behind his boots. It was like pushing a bull! The Zealot was not going to give any ground. Not even a step.

Angling his sword acutely in his right hand, Phoelius stabbed blindly around his shield, hoping to draw blood from the flanks or upper leg...

However, Loesheron sensed the shift in the knight's stance and slid aside to disengage. With a long stride backward, he set himself in a deep crouch, sword horizontal and pointed at the knight's eyes.

Phoelius lunged through the air with sword raised over his head! As it came thundering down, the Zealot's longsword greeted it with a loud, clear, chime of steel edges. Bright white sparks flashed between the speeding swords. Phoelius' one-handed slices, unparried, could have taken both arms off the Volgothan in a blink.

Like a black cyclone, the Volgothan spun, delivering a flurry of strikes to send Phoelius behind his shield. The Alcimaean was well-drilled, tireless, and strong... but also predictable. When the knight brought his shield directly in front of himself, the Volgothan grabbed the top rim. With a loud snarl, he slammed the base point down into the ground and vaulted himself over the top!

The kick to the face sent Phoelius rolling to the side through the tall red grass, his shield left behind like a gravestone in the field. He got a knee under himself and lifted his head, but then quickly ducked a swing of the Zealot's sword that would have left his skull fragments buried into the tree trunks.

Phoelius tumbled back and skittered on his knees and heels. The Volgothan followed, cloak billowing like he was a vulture descending on its meal.

"What's the matter, Alcimaean?" the Zealot spat. "Frightened of so fragile a creature?" His green eyes were wild with bloodlust. They shuddered, hardly blinking from the exciting thought of a kill.

The knight's glove tore shreds of papery bark from one of the white birches as he pulled himself clumsily to his feet. A broad uppercut of the longsword raked across Phoelius' chest, sending a spray of red hot sparks into the air. The blow wasn't powerful enough to cut through the white steel plates, but it knocked the knight off-balance. Phoelius stumbled back, and saw his dark adversary recoiling from the blow as well.

Instead of fighting to stay standing, Phoelius let himself fall, rolling forward and into Loesheron's legs!

The towering Volgothan staggered a long step forward. With a howl, Phoelius rushed and swung for the hand that gripped that terrible longsword...

The woods rang with the Volgothan's shout of pain, like the sounding of a church bell.

Loesheron staggered back a step, clutching his bloody ungloved hand. Phoelius couldn't help but freeze at the chilling roar, at the urge to flee like someone who has wounded a raging beast. A great wind from the east swirled through the trees, and the air was suddenly filled with hundreds of falling golden leaves.

"Yield, and return to your land," Phoelius said. "There is no dishonor—"

But the Zealot merely grit his teeth in a deep growl, tore Phoelius' shield from the ground where it stood, and charged.

Phoelius lowered himself to bear the blow. When his feet left the ground, he realized suddenly his mistake: the Volgothan's strength was even greater in his rage.

He saw double for a moment when his back struck the birch tree. His eyes bulged. Searing pain shot through his shoulder blades. Phoelius did not even feel his feet touching the ground again, and he fought to straighten his knees.

Loesheron flew knee-first, putting all his weight into a strike to the Alcimaean's breastplate. He heard a loud crack as the blow caught the knight with his back against the tree. Then, he went for Phoelius' sword.

The world was swirls of yellow and bursts of blue under Phoelius' eyelids as he reeled, but he felt the Volgothan tearing at his sword hand with blood-slicked fingers. He squeezed his hand tightly around the hilt. Breathing was a labor. He sucked in a gasp of air, and sharp pain shot through his chest as his vision cleared again. He felt his wrist twisting sharply from the Volgothan trying to wrench open his grip. His arm was trapped, locked down between the Zealot's folded arm and the black scales of his cuirass. One hand pried at Phoelius' fingers, and the other pressed mightily against the crossguard. Zealot Loesheron hissed, foaming through his grit teeth.

The trees overhead spun in Phoelius' vision. He staggered, legs weak, and put a hand to the Zealot's shoulder to shove himself free. Loesheron answered by driving his elbow back into the knight's face!

Phoelius' lips smashed against his teeth. His ears roared with adrenaline. His body flung itself backward in recoil. He tasted blood. Hot, chunky blood. Phoelius looked down at his fingers, at the skin peeled back into raw, white shreds where the Volgothan had clawed the sword out of his grip.

Zealot Loesheron rose, turning the shortsword over in his uninjured hand, as if testing the balance of the weapon. His serpentine gaze moved from the sword to the knight. A smile crept onto his face as he stalked forward.

Phoelius panted like a wounded dog. Dark blood flowed from his broken lips in long strands. His enemy had the upper hand, clearly, but was underprepared for this fight. He carried no secondary weapons...

As he backpedaled, Phoelius reached his right hand back behind his hip. His ungloved fingers felt along the leather belt fastened at his waist. They found the cold metal knobs of two throwing knives concealed in flat sheaths.

Loesheron charged. Phoelius threw the first knife. The Zealot saw it coming, and turned his torso so that it glanced off the black scales of his chestplate.

The second stuck into the vambrace guard protecting his elbow. If it wounded him, it did not slow him down.

Phoelius charged, going low for Loesheron's waist. The Volgothan lifted the sword for a two-handed, overhead chop that would split Phoelius open if he were holding his own longsword. But he was not. And while the chop was fast, Phoelius was faster. He lunged a step to the side and pounced with a third knife in his hand! He stabbed for a joint, hoping to break through a weak spot—

Instead, Loesheron's fist cracked across his already-bloody mouth, sending Phoelius spinning. He came to a stop at the base of a tree and knelt, clutching his side.

The red grass rippled around him chest-deep as he knelt there. Golden leaves, whirling in the wind, rained down around him. His mouth stung and bled freely now. His chest heaved painfully. Phoelius winced and then looked up to watch his executioner approach. He couldn't help but cough out a laugh.

The Zealot of Cannirath stood over him, sword in hand.

The Alcimaean smiled, "I can still offer you mercy."

"Mercy is a currency I do not deal in."

Phoelius watched as he, with cold resolve, lifted the sword.

There was a flash of metal through the air as Phoelius flung the fourth and last of his throwing knives, from its holster where he clutched his side.

The Zealot twisted backward, for in his right eye the knife had found its mark. His dark figure fell soundlessly in the crimson stalks. Quietly, birds began to chirp and call again in the treetops.

Phoelius groaned. He leaned his head against the tree, panting to catch his breath. This was not what he came here to do. There was debt to be repaid and justice to be done. Justice, not malice. Bracing with both hands, he pushed away from the tree, and retrieved his sword from where it lay.

He looked over the shining blade as it reflected the golden leaves overhead. His eyes did not look upon the fallen Volgoth, for there was no pride in their battle. There was only a thief to be brought back.

A thief who was long gone, leaving only a loop of rope behind.

Phoelius took a few steps in one direction, then in another. He was sure he could find the trail, but his ribs ached with each breath. The blood was drying on his chin. A glint of dark steel in the tall grass caught his eye.

Carrying the Zealot's longsword, he limped back to the middle of the glade and knelt down.

"Up, Zealot of Cannirath, if you yet draw breath for your King. Palepalm Grudgepost is the last place to get a mount for the ride northward. We can make it there by sunrise tomorrow. But first, there's a camp not far from here with a fresh leg of lamb waiting. Up, and let us be going."

THE WRONG BUSINESS

I t was the month Arca in Hellscry, the northernmost town in the territories of the immortal Ever-King of Volgoth. Snow-topped fir trees stood like dark, impenetrable walls all around the winding caravan trails, which were hewn out centuries ago by ogre grudges making their way south to trade. Though the Volgoth Empire had been broken years ago in the Silvanian Revolution, these trails were still essential for trade with the ogre grudgelands and beyond.

Deep in the forest was Jaded Lake: ice-cold, and reflective as polished steel. Frozen vegetation branched across its surface like black veins. Nearby was Jaded Lake Tavern, built around the base of one of the largest trees in the region. The tavern was a den for hunters of all kinds.

Fowl and deer hunters were everywhere at this time of the year, but in the forest trails north of Hellscry lurked a different sort of hunter: manhunters. While a typical huntsman could be hired for anything that required muscle and weapons, manhunters specialized in tracking individual targets to retrieve or eliminate them. Hiring a manhunter was illegal in the noble gleaming cities of Alcimaea, but here in Volgoth, nobody would bat an eye.

Two dozen patrons sat dining in the tavern. Built of long fir logs, it was six-sided in shape, with a huge tree that rose through the ceiling directly in the center and provided a canopy against harsh weather. The overcast daylight that filtered between the log walls began to wane.

Idly tapping her fingernails on the bar rail, Louella looked out at the waning daylight. It gleamed in her eyes, one of which was blue as the summer sky while the other was green as a meadow. Her gaze was attracted to the new glows of red lanterns and candles lit across the tavern. From there, her gaze began to wander.

In the corner was the dark silhouette of a Wolfkin nursing a flagon, cloaked by the hazy light coming in the wall slats behind it. Louella then traced the smell of meat over to the hearth, where several birds were spitted and roasting. At the hearth two men in leather tailcoats stood holding dripping bottles, taking swigs and exchanging words in a very intense conversation. The familiar smell of burnt meat and ale filled Louella's nose, and her stomach growled. Another hunter walked past — a hunched bald man in fur armor, with flesh the color of the snow outside. He was probably from the sunless frozen lands north of Wolvmonte. The albino growled and continued walking.

Just then, the tavern door creaked open noisily. A squat, wide-set woman with her black hair drawn back into a knotted bun on top, ambled in the doorway. A black owl sat on her shoulder, its eyes shut as if napping. She walked with a limp, and her almond-shaped eyes glared at other patrons as a warning to give her space. It was clear she was not one to be trifled with.

Louella turned away from the rabble of the hunter's den and sighed. Her last two hunts had been unsuccessful. She was looking for a win, but her competition always seemed a step ahead. Anger started to stir up in her. She licked her lips, rubbing together the last three gold coins in her pocket. A lock of her black hair fell down over her face. Suddenly, she slapped her hand down hard on the bar and glared at the barkeep, who hadn't so much as looked at her since she arrived. "HEY! What's a woman got to do to get a damn drink around here, huh?"

Huffing loudly, she saw out the corner of her eye the two men at the hearth looking at her with a chuckle. The huntress lifted the lock of hair away and tucked it behind her ear. The tavern patrons just murmured and returned to their business.

"Aye, right that. A woman who demands her worth," said the squat woman with the owl. The sudden comment in her hoarse voice startled Louella, who was clearly too on-edge.

After a hard sigh, a small smirk tugged on Louella's lips. She turned to the woman and admired the beautiful black owl first, before meeting her eyes. "Damn right indeed."

"What's your name?"

The huntress kicked the next stool out for her, inviting her to sit. "Louella... and you?"

"Faline," she replied and grunted as she eased herself down onto the seat. The black owl cocked its head, blinking its yellow eyes. The middle-aged woman stroked her gloved hand over the owl and then brought it to her jowled chin. "You don't look like a deer hunter. You've a cloak but no bow. You after someone?"

The barkeep, finally noticing the glint of Louella's coin on the bar, set a cup of house ale in front of her.

"I'm after a lot of things I've looked for and not found," she said before gulping down a long drink of ale. With her head tilted back, her hood fell. Long wavy black hair tumbled out, several curly locks falling over her face. Louella rolled her eyes and tossed the stray locks back. "What about you? How's the catch been?"

"Not so good," said Faline, a very thin smile creeping onto her face as she studied the young huntress. She did not break eye contact. "Been following a trail for two days. Normally I try to pace myself and let my prey do the running till they can't anymore. All things need to rest, as I'm sure you're aware?"

"Then what's the reason for the limp?"

She answered with a knowing look and a very subtle nod. It was obvious she wasn't hunting small game herself. "I got too close and my prey nipped me. Just enough to force me here, to stop and heal a bit."

Louella raised her eyebrows at the woman while gulping down more of her cold ale. The owl cocked its head to the side, and Louella mimicked its movement to entertain the bird. "Well, that is unfortunate indeed. All things *do* need to rest, including you it seems."

"A rest, and perhaps fresh eyes on the hunt." Louella coughed on the ale. "Oh no. Listen, I'm not chasing your prey into a quarry just for you to make off with them and leave me."

"Nothing like that," the elder huntress replied, leaning close. "Look, I had an original target out of Hellscry. Find-and-retrieve. My target was heading north into these woods. I was less than an hour behind, but then I suddenly lost the trail completely. Only tracks I could find were bigger... not hers. Someone else took her or left her. I searched but found nothing, and then I was ambushed. Arrow to the leg. It took me time to treat my wound and wrap it, and then I followed the tracks to the road. I lost time and ended up losing the trail. Only place the road could lead is here... Jaded Lake."

"Maybe another hunter got her? The woods are swarming with them."

"She's still practically a child. Most manhunters wouldn't even suspect this one."

"But you would?"

"It was a private contract."

"Fancy," Louella slurped at the last foam in her empty pint. "So something big and hungry took out your prey and you want me to throw myself to it? Nothing doing."

The barkeep returned, and Louella placed another gold coin on the counter to buy a second pint. Faline slapped her hand over Louella's to grab the coin. Like a tensed spring, Louella sprung up with a long dagger in her other hand. The two women froze.

Louella's stomach growled.

"I don't think something hungry got her. I think you're hungrier," Faline grinned.

"Is it that obvious?" in a shuddering laugh.

"Look, I'm not trying to trick you. I've got to rest here. Bring her back and I'll pay you half of my bounty. I'm hiring you, manhunter. This is the job I'm offering, and if you don't like it, go ahead and spend your last coins on ale and sleep on the bartop tonight."

Louella's eyes scanned the tavern. She saw a room full of cutthroat competition that would gladly leave her dead in a ravine than split a bounty. When Faline lifted her hand away, Louella held up the coin to the barkeep.

"Another ale," she grinned. "For my thirsty friend here. She'll be resting awhile."

Faline returned the grin. They had a deal.

Louella pushed the fresh cold pint over to her. "Never thought I'd be hired by another manhunter. Tell me more about my target... the one that took *your* target."

"The pup's barely full-grown but probably your size," lifting the ale and taking a sip.

"Pup? You're hunting a Wolfkin?" Louella whispered, eyes wide.

"The prints were definitely wolf prints. I caught sight of it before the arrow struck me. Tan flesh and auburn mane. I couldn't think of anywhere it or I could go, but here to Jaded Lake. Clearly, it's nowhere around now. It would be much faster on foot, so it must have beaten me to the lake and then moved on. I'm thinking it's headed to Palepalm Grudgepost at the border of the wilderness. If it passes there, you'll never catch it... and I'll never find her."

The young huntress listened intently, pushing another stray black lock behind her ear. Her mind was racing, trying to form a plan to catch up to a Wolfkin. It would easily move twice her speed. Just then, she remembered.

Louella spun and looked back to the spot where she'd seen the Wolfkin in the corner.

It was gone, the flagon still on the table.

"You know what?" she gasped, sliding off the stool, "It's getting pretty dark out and I don't want to waste a minute! I'll see you back here soon!"

The door to Jaded Lake Tavern banged against the wood column, rattling the lantern hung from it. Louella panted, her boots sliding in the snow outside. She looked this way and that.

"Bruid, up!" she called. From beside the column rose a huge black glariff: a wild hound subjugated by the Volgothans centuries ago into a guard and hunting dog. Glariffs were hairless, muscular as horses and nearly as tall — rising four feet high at the shoulder — with chests like barrels and tiny middles. His eyes were pale, lidless, pupilless orbs that topped his long, wrinkly head.

The pair walked into the snowy trail. There were indeed large pawprints she could see headed north, but the sun was nearly set. By the time she even followed them to the tree-line of the deep woods, it would be too dark to see them.

She squinted into the twilight and grit her teeth in frustration. She'd need both Bruid's speed and his sight on this one. The huntress knelt beside the hulking glariff and showed him the tracks, instructing him to seek and follow. She patted his snout in encouragement and then swung her leg over his back.

"I hope you don't mind giving me a ride," she muttered, hardly believing herself she was about to ride her hunting dog.

With but Louella's command "Find it," Bruid charged down the trail, following the footprints. Louella yelped, nearly sliding off as he accelerated with each stride of his long legs. She clung to his shoulders as they went. The tracks eventually broke off the road and into the woods.

The huntress barely had time to yank down on her hood trying to keep it down. Her curly black locks would easily tangle on any low hanging foliage and tear her off Bruid's back!

The pair charged through the forest with spectacular speed. The huge firs grew close together. More than once Bruid leapt between two narrow trees, scraping his shoulders and Louella's knees against the bark on either side. It was the glariff's relentless haste that made them such fearsome hunters, who chase their prey wherever it may go. Glariffs had been observed lunging after nesting seabirds, catching the birds in midair and then falling together down into the sea.

Suddenly, the loud crack of a projectile striking a passing tree made Louella hunker lower on her hound's back! *What was that?*

She was rounding another thicket when a second projectile struck, this time in Bruid's shoulder! She gasped as she saw the shaft of the arrow protruding from his flesh...

"Bruid! NO!" Louella shouted as Bruid stumbled and then fell.

The huntress bent over him to assess the wound. It had not gone deep, but enough to bring him down with the pain. She could treat him, but there was no time right now. Another arrow went by, sticking in the snow ten feet to her right.

She clenched her teeth and drew her long dagger. The angle of the arrows gave away the Wolfkin's position. She could not lose it now.

Her boots dug into the soft snow as she charged as fast and hard as she could. The Wolfkin was not fleeing when it could move so much faster. It wanted a fight, and Louella was more than happy to oblige.

The moon emerged from the clouds, casting white moonlight brightly between the firs. She saw the silhouette of the beastman against the light, and she darted for it! Instead of charging at her, it ducked and fled! Louella continued to charge through the strands of white moonlight after her prey, leaping over logs and crashing through brittle shrubs. The Wolfkin turned back at her and released another arrow, which went terribly wide of its mark.

The Wolfkin stumbled as it ran, and Louella was catching up to it. Perhaps Faline was right... all things need to rest and cannot run forever. Once she caught it, Louella would get the information on the girl and then slit its throat for hurting Bruid. Perhaps she'd even sell the pelt...

Clouds of vapor escaped between her teeth. She was nearly within reach of the fleeing Wolfkin now. Louella stepped up onto the next log and pushed off it to dive for the Wolfkin's tail! She came down with a firm grip on it, and she twisted her body to yank it off its feet.

Instead, Louella slid on the snow, holding onto the tail of a massive wolf's pelt.

A young human girl, no more than sixteen or seventeen summers, spun from the force of the furs being yanked off her. She fell awkwardly into the snow and cried out as she tried to get her footing again. She wore a wolf headdress, with the erected ears that Louella had seen in the tavern and again in the moonlight...

"YOU!" Louella shouted.

"The borderland is just a few miles north," the girl's voice trembled. The air was cold and misty. The girl fumbled with her satchel... "Please. I will give you all the gold I have if your mercy has a price."

Louella blinked in disbelief. She held up her dagger and stalked forward, unsure how to proceed. *It doesn't matter Louella, do your damn job,* she told herself.

The girl pleaded breathlessly, exhausted from running. "Please... please let me go. Not that you care, but they'll kill me—"

"You're right, I don't care." Louella snarled as she approached. The cold steel of her dagger shone between the moonlight above and the snow below, and she pointed it at the girl's throat. This girl had gone to all the trouble of fleeing and then throwing off her pursuer with a wolf pelt suit for a disguise. At a distance, she would appear as a fierce Wolfkin, and anyone with sense in their heads would keep a furlong between themselves and such a beast. "Who are you, and who are you running from?"

Okay, maybe I do care.

The girl's lip quivered, but something in her eyes showed unwavering determination. "I'm a runaway, from my family. Heading into the northlands to join my... well...." biting at her lower lip, "He's special to me."

Louella's dagger quivered as her grip on it loosened.

The girl set her jaw, and slowly stood up, eye-to-eye with her pursuer. She held in one hand a shortbow, and in the other a brown leather satchel. She took a short breath and slowly held out the satchel. "Four hundred gold, cold and counted. It's yours. Just please, give me the fur and leave me be, hunter," her voice breaking just at the very end of her sentence.

Louella did not move, save for her eyes lowering to the satchel and then back up. "Is it stolen?"

"All that I have is stolen," the girl replied in an embittered tone. "My family made no secret that everything I had in life, including the clothes on my back, was not mine to call my own. Not the home I was born in, or even the breath in my lungs, could be enjoyed without a reminder I was in their debt. That pelt I wear is the only thing keeping me alive… Bought with my own money, it is the only thing truly my own and no one else's, like my freedom."

The huntress' heart sank. Nevertheless, she squeezed her dagger all the tighter and took a step closer, touching it lightly to the girl's collarbone. "What a brave little dove. All of this trouble, and for what? For a man? So young, so pretty, and so… stupid."

The girl swallowed a lump in her throat. She did not dare look at the cold steel at her neck.

Louella stepped nose to nose with the girl and in a low growl said, "I ought to kill you right here out of sheer pity. If they want you dead, I can save everyone the trouble. Give me one good reason I shouldn't just take your gold and let my dog gnaw your corpse like a beef bone."

"I haven't a reason for you," her voice a stiff whisper in the night air. "That gold was going to get me a mount, but now I'll be forced to walk the badlands on foot."

Louella's icy demeanor nearly broke. She knew someone with the same will, the same determined spirit once before... one she used to see in mirrors, looking back at her.

The runaway shuddered in the cold as she put a hand to the wolf fur pelt in Louella's arms. Her voice was now quite still, no longer trembling. "Whether it were for a man, a fortune, or a flower... would it matter which? I freed myself, and I can again if I must. I will always be free."

A lock of Louella's black hair fell between her eyes. She attempted to move it with a toss of her head, but it stubbornly clung to the perspiration. The huntress' mismatched eyes of blue and green shimmered in the moonlight. They lowered to look at the fur pelt, with the girl's hand resting gently upon it.

Louella put the dagger back, sighed, and shoved the pelt into the girl's hands. "Foolish little girls dream of happy endings," she said as she pushed back the lock of hair. "If you've chosen badly what to do with your freedom, your punishment will find you all by itself."

The young girl stared in disbelief, taking a step backward and throwing the fur around her shoulders once more. Unable to find any more words, she shakily held out the satchel.

Louella snatched it. Inside were four small sacks of gold coins. "I pity you. This will just about pay for my trouble. Now run off before I change my mind and sic Bruid on you."

The girl backed away, unsure whether to thank the huntress or not. Silence and gold was payment enough to keep her freedom. She stared a moment longer, nodded, and then ran. The last Louella saw of her was the shape of a wolf escaping in the flashes of broken moonlight.

There was a low whine as Bruid came slowly to his master's side. Louella patted his head and scratched behind his ear. He huffed up at her and sat on the ground.

"The ogres at Palepalm Grudgepost will probably give her something in trade for that fine bow and the pelt. She may not ride to her lover on a horse, but she just might show up on a stork-legged poradon or a scampering queed if they have one big enough."

The pair turned and plodded back to find the forest trail. Bruid snarled.

"I know, I know... We're in the wrong business."

THE CROSSING

The woodland was silent until the sound of crushing snow broke the calm of sunset. A cloaked figure pushed through the deep snow, with strands of crimson hair escaping the hood and dancing in the soft breeze. Breathing heavily, the woman turned to look back. Her hood fell back for a moment, letting her long hair tumble onto her shoulder. A stream of blood ran down the side of her face from her temple. It was not her only wound. As she ran along through the snow, she was leaving a trail of blood behind her. A small cry urged the woman to face forward. She clutched the small bundle in her arms.

"Hush little one..." her voice soft, she gently placed a finger on the infant's smooth cheek to soothe the babe. The woman flinched slightly as the pain in her side grew worse. Knowing she didn't have long, she pressed on.

Come on Eirene... you cannot fall yet... the words echoing in her mind. She told herself again and again, at the bottom of every hill and at the deepest part of every snowdrift. *You cannot fall yet.* Between that in the babe in her arms, it gave her the strength to continue.

As the sun set further, the shadows of the tall lines grew longer, covering them in darkness.

A small white light pierced the darkness. Eirene held a glowing dagger in her small hand, waving it between the trees. She now felt only a few inches of snow around her boots, for the snow became thinner as the woods grew thicker. Coughing as she covered her mouth with her sleeve, she clenched her eyes at the metallic taste in her mouth. Eirene mouthed a curse as she pulled back to see blood. The cold wind wailed through the treetops. Tears welling in her eyes, she looked down at the babe in the crook of her arm.

Soft grey eyes — like her father — looked up at Eirene. She smiled softly at her child but that slowly turned into a frown.

"My dear little one... I'm sorry I have gotten you into danger." She leaned against the trunk of a nearby tree. Wrapping the cloak around herself and her small babe, she drew in a few short breaths. She tied the ends of her cloak around her waist to make a sling for the child. It would shelter her in the warmth of the cloak as long as possible.

Eirene leaned her head against the tree a few seconds longer before she pushed herself off it. She lifted the glowing dagger in her free hand and drove it into the trunk. Eirene looked away into the woods, watching the shadows cast on the trees by the light of the enchanted blade above her.

She winced again, holding her side. "A simple spell caused me this much pain. He must have done more than what I thought at first," she spoke as she wearily stared into the darkness around them. As she watched the tree line, she felt her eyelids growing heavier the longer she sat there. Her eyes closed for a few moments...

The sound of crunching caused her eyes to open with a shudder. *Am I awake or adream?* Someone was drawing closer to her. Was it he that pursued her? Eirene tried to get up, but she had no strength in her tired legs folded beneath her. She cursed and she looked down at her babe hidden in her cloak, holding her close as a figure slowly appeared out of the shadows.

A loud snarl followed, and a booming voice was heard. "What are you doing here, human? Foolish woman. It is death to enter our land."

A Wolfkin.

Steam streamed out of his muzzle in the cold. His eyes flared, reflecting the light of the dagger glowing on the tree trunk. The Western Woods were forbidden for humans. The Wolfkin's hatred for them was bred through decades of war for territory and power.

Eirene coughed softly, and she pushed herself to lean up a little. Her long red hair was tangled and covered in snow. "I was only passing through..." Her voice was hoarse.

She watched as the amber eyes grew closer, and the beastman walked into the small dim light. He stood nearly eight feet tall and was covered in thick, shaggy black fur that billowed between the sections of his leather armor plates.

About his neck was a roughspun mantle that further shielded him from the biting cold. A feeling of helplessness overtook her. She knew she could not fight him. If he raised a sword or claw against her, she would certainly perish.

"Passing through? You don't look like you are going much farther," in a grim growl. "You smell of death. It clings to you like a whelp..." he scoffed as he watched the young woman pull her cloak closer to her.

Eirene looked up at him and glared, but said nothing as his words rang true. She resisted looking down into her cloak at the babe in her hands.

"Then as death is coming for this foolish woman finally... could you do one thing..." she asked with a weak smile on her face.

The Wolfkin snorted slightly as he loomed over her, "To bring your suffering to an end? That I can do. But I feel that is not what you will ask." His eyes were drawn to what she held so closely in her hands.

A soft laugh escaped the woman. It was followed by a cough and blood dripping down from the corner of her lips. She looked up at him. "You are a smart wolf. I may not have much time left, but my daughter does. My little Avonlea is strong… and will make it through when her mother cannot."

She coughed as she pulled the hem of the cloak back, and gently played with her child's soft red curls.

"You expect me to take this child... a human babe?" The Wolfkin's lips snarled back in laughter until something caught his attention: the air grew thick with mist around them, and the glimmering beams of green light that shone in the mist.

The Wolfkin took a few steps backward, looking around. He fumbled for the large jagged weapon on his belt and turned back to Eirene. His eyes widened as he beheld her. Her tired eyes, now fogged over and white, stared as the woman whispered words he could not understand: a forbidden enchantment.

She lifted her hand up to her forehead. The light around them grew brighter as she chanted. The last of her strength and power would be spent. Wiping the blood from her forehead with her finger, she gently pressed it on her daughter's forehead. The light then grew brighter, so that even the fierce Wolfkin had to shield his eyes.

Eirene smiled down at her daughter sadly. "My dear Avonlea... I may not be able to watch you grow, but I will protect you." Tears were running down her face as she closed her eyes. "And by doing this, the hunter will never find you."

Then, she spoke the final words of the enchantment. With a smile on her face, she looked upon her sweet child for the last time...

The shining beams suddenly disappeared, leaving them all in darkness.

The Wolfkin opened his eyes, at last, blinking to focus his night vision. He lumbered forward with a weapon in hand. "Witch! What trick do you think you are playing! I will not be your slave, your midwife!" he snarled until he looked upon the woman — a smile on her pale face, and a stream of tears frozen in place.

He backed away a step, startled then by the crunch of his own footstep in the snow. Crouching down on all fours, he approached. Eirene sat there against the tree, holding the bundle against her still chest. The Wolfkin placed his paw against her cheek.

Her skin was cold... She was gone.

A small cry caught his attention, and he turned his amber gaze down at the bundle. Slowly he took the small babe in his large claws. Being gentle with her, he lifted her up to look at her. He saw soft reddish-brown fur and tiny paws reaching up to him — a Wolfkin pup, her soft grey eyes filled with curiosity.

The huge Wolfkin looked at the mother and then at the child. He rose slowly, turning and walking away toward the dark of the woods. He took off his roughspun mantle and began to clumsily swaddle her in it...

The crack of wood splitting raised the Wolfkin's hackles as he whirled about. Eirene's dagger, still softly aglow, was now held in a gloved hand plated with white steel.

"You are lucky to be alive," the armored hunter called out. "A witch's curse can only be cast with her dying breath. She could have turned you into a pillar of salt, or plagued the whole forest with pestilence." He reached down and took hold of the dead woman's tangled locks to look her in the face.

The Wolfkin stayed silent as the hunter spoke. He held the babe close and turned away.

"I'll be burning the corpse. I won't be long," the deep baritone echoed in the glen.

The Wolfkin grimaced but kept walking. "See that you are not, hunter. I am not the only one who guards our borders."

Avonlea pawed at the mantle, trying to look behind them at the fading light. She could not scale the thick fur of his shoulder and gave up. A moment later, a different light captured her attention: the shine of the moon between the parting clouds in the night sky. The little one cooed and laid back, watching the moonlight.

"Saved by your curse. I'll keep her alive..." was the last thing he said as he returned to the shadows, with the small bundle in his arms.

SCORN FOR THE SPARROW

Oczandarys' strong, clear voice shattered the silence of the house.

"I don't recall extending an invitation."

Juhadiel whirled around with a start, dropping the white apple he was admiring. Several plates of fruit, atop thin poles several feet high, stood around Oczandarys' audience chamber. The room was immense, with pillars eighty feet high and vaulted ceilings barely visible in shadow. On all sides beyond the pillars lay the gleaming landscape of the Angelic realm.

"I don't recall requiring one," Juhadiel replied, his red wings folded neatly behind himself. His robes were crimson and white and flowed in a long train behind him. He tossed his auburn locks and stood straighter.

He could never feel totally at ease around Oczandarys, despite their close companionship over the centuries. Oczandarys had many fellows but hardly friends. Perhaps it was the way the tall, bronze-skinned Angelic held himself, decked in ornamented armor as if never truly letting his guard down. Perhaps it was the patterns of ink seared into his skin, symbolizing his long life without rebirth. Without rebirth, his skin bore every blemish and scar, as did his mind.

The latter blemishes and scars were Juhadiel's preoccupation.

Oczandarys strode in, stepping past the fallen white apple and locking eyes with his friend. "Invitation to dine, not to visit," the master of the house quipped. "I leave for an hour and already the mice come to nibble?"

Juhadiel smiled reassuringly. "Curiosity, not appetite, drew me to call upon you."

"Appetite can be filled at least. Curiosity has no limits."

A moment that seemed longer than most passed. Oczandarys sat down in one of the tall-backed white chairs in the chamber. There was no dias, no throne, no central seat upon which he ever sat. Juhadiel had always observed, in fact, that in hundreds of years it seemed Oczandarys never so much as favored a chair over others in his house.

"You have always been an odd one, Oczandarys. Where your brothers and sisters have always been singular you have been plural. They focus upon a single task, while you dwell upon many. They enlist a single mortal, while you command a host."

The bronze Angelic sat still as stone. "And this troubles you?"

Juhadiel's wry grin shifted to a smirk of true amusement. "What troubles me is a sudden single-mindedness I now observe in my dear friend."

"Oh?"

"Concerning a certain little sparrow who recently fell from grace..."

"Nonsense!" Oczandrys now stirred from his chair, standing as if he was a valley becoming a mountain. His immense black wings stretched, their tips trailing the smooth, shiny floor. "The loss of her grieved me but I had even now misplaced her name for a moment."

Juhadiel slowly stepped closer, his palms together. "Ah. But it's not her name upon which you dwell. Is it?"

"I know not your meaning."

"You do."

"I swear that I do not."

Juhadiel drew back a step and nodded. "Then it was not Suzura's face in the mindglass you gazed upon yesterday."

"It matters not if it was," with a flippant tone.

"And it matters not that you were not gone an hour, but nearly a day."

Oczandarys' golden eyes now met Juhadiel's. They narrowed slightly and his lips twitched into a curt smile.

"Next time that I venture so long, I will tell you ahead of time the hour of my return."

"Will you?"

"I will," smiling and putting his hand to Juhadiel's shoulder as he walked him out of the audience chamber. "I don't like for you to have to linger so long. Anticipation pangs the appetite—oh, my error—*the curiosity*."

Juhadiel nodded knowingly. It was time for him to leave. Oczandarys' temple had no physical doors or bars, but the passage he awaited was definitely locked tight.

"Thank you, my friend. I'll see you again soon." Spreading his red wings, Juhadiel departed across the sky.

The master of the house returned beneath the shadows of the pillars and to the side of his chair. He looked down at the white apple that lay on the floor beside him.

Gently, he laid his foot upon it. Then, he crushed it.

~

The red-winged celestial streaked across the sky — through vaporous archways, over rolling domes, and past rows of titanic pillars between crackling thunderheads. Far below were the plains and seas of Grimmgard, visible to him only briefly between the clouds.

He stepped onto a flat sheet of vapor and then retreated beneath the massive shelf of dark cloud, down a set of stairs, and into his sanctum. Small floating orbs of divine light drifted lazily as snowflakes in the dim chamber to offer their radiance where needed.

"Juhadiel!"

He shut his eyes before slowly turning to face her. The tall, statuesque woman flounced down the sanctum stairs after him.

Her eyes were the color of jade, and her wavy hair bright as the purest pearl.

"Oczandarys gave *you* an audience?" she asked curtly.

"Only just."

Her fists clenched at her sides as she burst out, "Am I *so loathed*? Am I such abhorrent company that I am thus shunned, and always have been? Am I so noxious a companion to merit this treatment from him?"

"Nandrzael, you know that is not the case. All things past and all things future, pass before him. His mind is far afield, and you know it must needs be so."

"Were he preoccupied with the future instead of the past, he would have attended the urgent business I have with him. But he vanishes for a day and tells no one. I wish I were so naive as to wonder why."

Juhadiel folded his red wings back till they touched each other. The feathers rippled and straightened themselves. "It is the loss of her that burdens him."

"Why, Juhadiel?" she pleaded, tears glistening in the jade. "Trifle not with me, for I am no child. What did Suzura possess that I did not, save for the heart of the one I desired? What possibly could his golden eyes have seen that fastened them upon *her* so steadily? She possessed no particular might, no gift, no anomaly of beauty greater than any of her kindred.

Yet blissfully, effortlessly, she captivated that which ever eluded me."

He had resisted up until now, but she deserved an answer from him. "Some things are easy... natural. It was not much between them at first: a few sought-out conversations here, a sideways glance or two there. Not many noticed as I did."

"I did too, but only as a fleeting fear. As one fears a flood when it has only begun to rain."

Juhadiel continued. "As you know, Suzura was not one of the originals created by the hands of the Makergods themselves. Neither were you, Nandrzael. She was not permitted to enter the greatest of our sanctuaries, to gaze into the mindglass, and there to see the futures of whomsoever she wished. Oczandarys, far older and wiser, looked on her behalf. Just as we are sworn to guide mortals with gifts and blessings without direct intervention, so did Oczandarys guide her."

"You make it seem so innocent, Juhadiel, like two saplings that grow alongside one another and wind their branches together year by year," she spat. "But I saw in every sought-out conversation, the way the violet in her eyes mingled with the gold in his. It was as though every time they spoke, they stood nearer and nearer one another."

"This story is no fanciful romance, for it has no heartwarming end. You see, she played patron to a mortal man whose destiny was tragedy, and in a moment of overwhelming compassion, drew her sword to intervene and save his life," Juhadiel explained, pain creeping into his voice. "Oczandarys had no choice but to take her before the council. Her sentence should have been something far worse, but Oczandarys bade the council to banish her instead. And thus, cut off from the regenerating power of our celestial realm, she is as mortal as any of those who walk the world below. She was cast out. Do you hear me? She is not coming back."

"And yet day after day he watches... he wants her back," tears rolling down her face.

"You do know not of what you speak—"

"I do..." her voice in shattered agony, "Something is missing in him. I see it in his eyes, like less gleam in the gold. I hear it in his voice, like an orchestra that has lost an instrument. I see it in his walk, like thunder without lightning, that wanders not knowing where to go."

Juhadiel's mouth hung agape. "You can see then, what others cannot. Beyond doors and bars that I myself fail to circumvent."

"I can see but I cannot reach," she rushed to him, squeezing his hands in hers. "Is it naught but this broken sparrow's tragic estate that draws his eye? Does the chiefest among us only have his heart affixed toward those who have fallen? Will he bow himself to the edges of the clouds and pine till time turns all to dust?"

Nandrzael shoved him angrily as she tore herself away from him, and faced away with her head in her hands. Her wings shimmered like crystal among the floating orbs of light in the sanctum.

The sullen silence broke with Juhadiel's low, resolute voice. "For millennia, my old friend has only preoccupied himself with the mission of thwarting the darkest evils that threaten lifekind. I cannot believe his feelings for her now can be anything but how to employ her further toward his mission. The evils beyond our world have always been his focus until now."

The jade-eyed Angelic's sigh echoed in the sanctum. Her very spirit ached like one's bones ache after walking and walking, and still not finding the way before darkness falls.

"Then they had best busy themselves to keep his focus in the future," she replied hollowly.

Her great crystal wings spread, and Nandrzael silently flew from the sanctum, never to return.

THE PRISONER

The city of Holireath was one of the oldest cities in all of Grimmgard. Its walls, turrets, and towers were made of polished stone, which glittered like gold in the daylight. The shape of the city was like unto a tree, for like a trunk the illustrious palace of the king towered at its center, and like roots dozens of archway-covered roads snaked out from the palace to the perimeter walls.

The cold, white winter sun glinted off the great brass gates of the perimeter walls as a wagon rumbled into the city. Between the perimeter and the inner walls lay vast open plazas filled with merchants from lands far and near: fur traders from the northeastern wilderness, jewelers from mysterious Khon Dha at the southern sea, and Dwarven merchants demonstrating their clockwork innovations. The wagon rumbled past and under the shadow of the inner gateway pavilion. Here at this massive station, all who entered had to be searched and approved by Holireath's guardsmen.

This wagon was simply waved through by the guardsmen, giving a nod of their horned black helmets to the driver. He proceeded under the portcullis, driving the wagon slowly toward the great palace.

The snowy streets were pulsing with activity. Dogs ran by the wagon wheels, yipping and barking at the pale mammoth pulling it along. The citizens made way, walking alongside it to maybe catch a glimpse of who stood clinging to the cage bars of the prison wagon. All they saw was a longcoat of black bearskin through the bars.

The wagon crossed the long drawbridge over the moat and vanished into the palace keep. The gates immediately slammed shut, and the drawbridge rose.

~

Six guardsmen stood around their prisoner. His hands and feet were bound with a set of iron shackles, but he had already broken the first set after being let out of the wagon. They were not taking any chances.

"Take off his hood," a voice called out from above them.

One of the guardsmen yanked the black hood off his head. A mess of dark hair fell to his shoulders, and a single green, snakelike eye opened.

He saw that he stood in the middle of a pillar-lined atrium of polished stone, with a circular cutaway in the ceiling above. A fountain about eight feet wide lay in the center of an atrium. Steam rose off the water that bubbled from the fount. Thriving in the warmth of the thermal spring water, ivy grew along the walls, out the cutaway, and up the arched support beams overhead. They formed a latticed dome, through which hazy daylight streamed down.

At the edge of the cutaway, peering down into the atrium, was a man wrapped in thick layers of royal blue robes with golden silk hems. His appearance was crowned with a steel helmet of incredibly ornate design: sculpted perfectly into the shape of a man's face, complete with brows, eyeholes, hair of chainmail, and even interlocking plates that formed a beard and curled mustache.

"You must be King Crispus," the prisoner called up to him.

The old king's voice was strong but calm, like a father imploring a son. "What evil have I done, that the Ever-King of Volgoth sends his servants to trouble my land, Zealot Loesheron?"

"It is my land that has suffered the evil. A certain thief and highwayman has evaded Volgoth justice and now has found sanctuary in Holireath. I will find him, and take him for judgment. Release me."

"This certain thief is one of my people?" the king asked.

"No, King Crispus, he is a man of Alcimaea, but his crimes have made him a fugitive from his own land. He has wrought a trail of bloodshed and havoc that I followed here. Release me."

"If reports are true, you've wrought a similar trail yourself, Zealot."

"I met with resistance during my search."

"Have you come alone, or have you brought others with you?"

The Zealot sneered. "I traveled with an Alcimaean knight by the name of Phoelius. We crossed the badlands northward in pursuit of the same man, and then lodged together in the inn at a village not far from here. I thought it wise to awaken early and ask the other lodgers if they had seen the man we pursued. Certainly the king can understand my urgency and forgive any imprudence."

"Two men dead is quite the imprudence."

"Four," one of the guardsmen interrupted. "He killed two of my men downstairs."

"Unarmed?"

"The shackles were all I needed," the Zealot replied.

"Your will is very strong," King Crispus remarked, folding his hands in front of him and pacing around the cutaway high above them. "It is said when the strong-willed die, they fight the current that pulls their souls to Avgannon for judgment. Instead, they remain here as wandering spirits... ghosts. If I were to order your execution, undoubtedly you would become such a doleful spirit."

"I too have heard such things. Ghosts hunt the living and feed on them to survive."

"Bound in my dungeon, you would freeze or starve, and eventually become a hollow: a hungering shell of a soul, scrounging for beetles and little white rats."

The Zealot scowled at first, but then grinned. "Beware, O King, for I have also heard that a ghost who escapes and feeds freely upon the living, will grow in strength to become a wroth: a demon of dreadful power."

King Crispus paused and slowly looked down at him. He had ruled Holireath for over a hundred years, and stood in judgment over many impenitent souls. He knew this Volgothan would not yield to conviction or threats.

"Release me," Loesheron repeated once more, forcefully.

The king laughed quietly under his iron helmet. "No. In my land, a violent beast gone astray from its master will be caught and chained until he is reclaimed. So, it must be with you."

With but a gesture of the king's hand, the guardsmen threw the black hood back over their prisoner's head. They seized his arms and dragged him out of the presence of the masked king.

~

The palace dungeons were not buried beneath the keep, but located in a tall tower overlooking the east side of the palace. This made escape virtually impossible: descending the tower stairs meant running into bottlenecked passages filled with guardsmen. The outer wall of each cell was a mesh of diagonally interlocking bars. Even if one could get through the bars, it was hundreds of feet down to the ground or — at best — the moat, which was filled with venomous waspfish that could sting through solid armor.

The dungeon level was freezing with the winter cold. In its center, hanging cages dangled at varying heights around the central stone column. The perimeter of the room was lined with two stories of cells. The mesh of bars on the outer wall allowed the biting wind to chastise the prisoners. The jailers worked in shifts to relieve each other from the conditions.

Loesheron slowly paced in his cell. Now shirtless, he had been stripped of his cloak and scaled armor, which presumably lay elsewhere with his weapons.

He kicked the metal pail over in his cell. "This is folly. I was the one wronged, and justice was meted out by my hand. I should be walking free, not wasting time here!"

"You killed two men and nearly killed a third," said the jailer, a big man with a thin goatee. He sat on a stool across from the Zealot's cell, pulling a woolen blanket closer around himself.

"Nearly? Then there I see my fault. I was sure my blade was sharp."

"I heard they had merely asked you to leave the inn."

"And I wasn't ready to leave until my questions were answered. I see not the fault there."

The jailer leapt up, the blanket and stool falling behind him. "You think you can just walk into another land, and treat it as if it were your own? This is Holireath, you black-heart. There are laws and customs that must be observed, even by outsiders. This is how peace prevails in our land. Lawless behavior cannot—"

"Lawless?" the prisoner objected.

"Yes, lawless! I don't know if you fancy yourself a warrior for justice or purely for hate and indignation. Your Volgoth is a land of evil and violence! No law contains what you do!"

Loesheron laughed in his cell, though his ire was beginning to kindle. "All that I do becomes the law. The Ever-King's supreme will ordains it."

"Is that why there is darkness and murder and hate in your land? Is that why brother turns against brother, or against sister, mother, and father, without trial? If your king's will is supreme, then why is it so?"

"It is so because that is his will!" the Volgoth's shout ricocheted around the dungeon walls. "You understand nothing. Is it so hard for you to accept, that what is vice to you may be law unto us? All are born and all die at the Ever-King's command, Jacorian. Our hearts only move by his breath — his very word! If he commands for gold, we will find it. If he commands for a new generation, we will bear it. And if he commands for the blood of our loved ones, we will wring it out! Look at you... your aging sovereign gives the law and you wrestle with it inside. You doubt. Every man with his morals, his own law in his heart, to lead him astray. It is not so in the lands of Volgoth. My land, where there are no jails for its own people. There is no conscience, no struggle. There is no remorse, no doubt, no debate! There is obedience... and there is power. His power, that spans the world."

"Not here. Here you do not have that power," the jailer replied, his voice shaking. "So long as these walls stand, your words are only prolonged by King Crispus' mercy."

"Then *your* power is naught but the stone, mortar, and metal that imprisons me." he smiled maliciously as he approached and reached through the bars as far as he could. "Your power spans only as far as the distance from my hand to your throat."

The jailer stood sweating and white as a sheet. His shriek echoed through the dungeon spire as a hand tapped him on the shoulder.

The next shift had arrived.

~

The cold day gave way to the frigid night. The dungeon was lit now only by clusters of lumpy candles set here and there on the stone floor. The jailer was reluctant to return for his overnight shift, keeping his distance from the Zealot by sitting back against the wall near the doorway to the stairwell. In an hour he had nodded off to sleep, arms crossed.

Loesheron had given up pacing by sunset. He now stood with his fingers curled in the mesh of metal bars, peering out at the city of Holireath below. From far away, a musical note from here would mix discordantly with another musical note from there. The distant symphony was like a ballad echoing from the bottom of the sea. He saw lanterns were lit in the streets for some reason. The Jacorians were making merry on this evening. It was Scöth Androdyd most likely, the sixteenth day of the month Arca.

He sighed. He had been hunting this certain thief since the robbery of a caravan coming into Cannirath more than two months ago. The duel with the Alcimaean knight had cost him his right eye, and the whole venture had cost much more in grief alone that could never be made back...

"Did I hear there is a Zealot in our midst?" a woman's voice crooned from the cell above him.

He paused in surprise. "You have heard rightly. I am Loesheron of Cannirath. You speak not after the manner of the northmen nor of the golden kingdom of Alcimaea. Who are you?"

"I am Talla... of His Majesty's imperial legion."

Loesheron's eyes widened. He grabbed the cell bars and pulled himself close. "An imperial knight? By the King, what are you doing here?"

"A month ago, the northern villages near Hellscry were struck by a renegade warlord — the third time in a moon cycle."

"A warlord?"

"Yes sire," the woman explained, "A great dark lionkin what calls himself Manticore."

Loesheron had heard of this creature. The bloodthirsty Manticore had killed several lords of Jacore in his quest for power and dominion. Foiled but never defeated, this lionkin was a terror in the northlands.

"Go on," he prompted Talla.

"The Great Inquisitor obtained a writ of passage from Rurik the Toothless that let us ride uninhibited from my home in Golgoshath all the way north to the shores of the Sea of Shadows. After six days' journey we discovered his encampment along the shores in the dead of night. We fell upon them, supposing to kill Manticore and his marauders while they slept. Instead, they ambushed us. They collapsed the cliffside and trapped the entire battalion on the shoreline. I was the only survivor."

"And me," a man's voice called from one of the hanging cages. A burly man sat curled inside it. His long, red, felted hair was visible even through the thick bands of his cage, as was his large, curly beard.

"Who is that?" Zealot Loesheron asked.

Talla answered, "Manticore's warband had two sorcerers. On his right hand was one called Darkmane, and on his left this man: Othric the Great."

"For the last time," the man's voice echoed from his cell, "It's '*aw-thrick*,' not '*oh-thrick*.' Back of the throat, Volgothan. '*Awwww-thrick*.'"

"My apologies. When we escaped without the Inquisitor's writ of passage, we became little more than renegades in the lands of Jacore. And so I was apprehended as a trespasser, along with *Oth*ric the Great," Talla amended, smiling as she stressed the first syllable of his name.

"You'd just as well drop the 'Great' part. There's nothing great about me," Othric lamented quietly.

"Don't start on yourself again."

"What troubles you?" the Zealot asked him.

"Darkmane channeled the mighty works of Chaos before our lord. I, on the other hand, was gifted with little more than the Feeric art of trickery and nonsense."

"Feeric sorcery? Does that not mean you possess power over luck… and miracles?"

Othric scoffed. "Sure. Fat lot of good it's done. Abandoned by my master and now locked in a dungeon tower shivering out of the last of my days with two crows pecking at my ears. It would be quite the miracle if all of us do not die in this loathsome place."

The Zealot watched him carefully. "Where are you from, Othric the Great?"

"The White Shores, eastward of the Mountain of Iron."

"The White Shores, where lie the ruins of the Guardian City and of Dimol Gol?" he asked, and then paused in thought. "That is quite a bloodline you boast, child of Mirikinin."

"Well, here I'm just vermin in a trap, and not for the first time," he said sullenly.

Talla knelt in her cell and spoke softly down to Loesheron. "Manticore's army left him as bait for the ambush. They abandoned him in the Black Shallows to die with us. It was not long before my fellow knights began vanishing into the night one by one. The *shallowmen* preyed upon us."

"Shallowmen?"

"Terrible wroths that rose from the shallows to seize us and drag us under the water, horse and rider together. It was only with luck that I was able to escape with my life."

"And with Othric too."

"Yes."

"Luck indeed," the Zealot commented thoughtfully and then turned to the man in the cage. "I think your powers may yet be of use, enchanter. Tell me, what all can you do?"

"I can enchant you so that if you tell a lie, a frog will leap from your mouth."

There was a long, prevailing silence.

"I hoped you'd have the power to transform into a hulking, two-headed giant or some such," the Zealot said.

"Not quite. But I can shrink myself to the size of a perching bird."

Another silence. "I may be able to make do with that. What else?"

"Well," Othric faltered for a moment. "I can fly, I think."

"You think?"

"My lord Manticore had very little use for a flying pocket sorcerer when Darkmane could summon fire from his eyes, collapse mountainsides, or open the ground to swallow his adversaries. I haven't had much practice."

"If you can shrink yourself and fly," Talla interjected, "Why have you not flown out of here? Slipped between the bars and out across the city to freedom?"

Othric groaned. "I have tried, believe me. The outer mesh bars are interlocked too tightly for me to get out. Nothing short of breaking them will free me of this prison, and I doubt either of you possess the strength to do so."

"Not with flesh and bone, but perhaps with something more," Loesheron said, lowering his voice to a hiss.

"What do you mean?"

He cast a glance at the sleeping jailer at the doorway and then back to Othric. "They have confiscated my armor and weaponry. Among them are two magic potions, kept in black leather casings on my sword belt. One of them is a blast potion."

"An explosive?" he whispered back. "Are you mad?"

"Hardly. Heed me, Othric. Use your enchantments to escape your cage and discover where they have stowed my armament. Return to me with the jailer's key while he yet sleeps."

There was silence from the cage. Loesheron ground his teeth waiting for Othric to answer. The jailer could wake at any time. They had gotten away with this conspiracy unnoticed so far, but their luck could not last forever.

"Do this, and you shall henceforth always be a friend to Volgoth," Loesheron urged him.

"You can do it," Talla added. Othric's cage creaked a little as he stirred.

Something in her voice made Loesheron realize these two were more than just survivors. It was not good fortune that delivered this disheartened man from death at the Black Shallows, it was Talla's compassion. She had not only spared his life but escaped with him, and traveled with him many days' journey back to Holireath. A man overshadowed by his rival, abandoned by his master, and rescued by an enemy he was meant to lure to her death? He did not need alliances or bargains. Poor Othric just needed encouragement.

"I believe in you," she whispered to him.

"Please," Zealot Loesheron added, shutting his eye. "Release me."

Across the dungeon, the sorcerer began to recite the incantations.

A surge of wind swept through the dungeon, snuffing out half the candles. Then, the walls glowed a deep hue as golden sparks swirled around the sorcerer! Othric's cage rattled and then settled, swinging creakily from its chain. Everything fell dark and quiet again.

The Volgothans blinked in the darkness before two tiny golden wings flickered like candlelight. Othric, small as a blackbird, darted through the air and down the stairs past the jailer.

With bated breath, they watched the doorway for the golden glow to return. A minute passed.

A moment longer than a minute, the glow of Othric's wings returned. The shrunken figure flew around the corner and then clumsily bounced into the jailer's chair leg, trying to latch onto it. The jailer did not stir.

Othric crept up the chair leg and to the ring of long iron keys hanging from his belt loop. Slowly as he could, he unhooked the heavy ring and hefted it onto his shoulder. With a flutter of his glittering wings, he floated back away from the jailer and then bobbed through the air over to the lock for Loesheron's cell.

The moment the key was firmly in the lock, Othric returned to normal size. Just as when he shrank, golden sparks flared and swirled around him!

The sleeping jailer's eyes clenched from the bright light and then flickered open. He sat forward groggily, hearing the squeal of the cell door.

His eyes bulged as Loesheron's hand gripped his throat. His legs kicked wildly as he was lifted high off the ground. The last thing he saw was his reflection in the Zealot's reptilian eye before the back of his head slammed into the wall. The jailer slumped to the floor, a smear of blood left on the wall behind him.

The Zealot of Cannirath stared coldly down at the body. "Now, where are my armaments?"

"The armory is three flights down, but there are four guardsmen along the way."

"Not for long."

Othric did not watch him vanish down the dark stairway. He ascended the walkway to the upper cell and unlocked it.

He and Talla fell into each other's arms. He ran his cracked fingers through her black hair and lost himself in the shine of her ivory-colored eyes. This was the longest they'd been apart since leaving the Shallows.

~

The first guardsman only saw a blurred shape of the Zealot lunging low beside him. He left the ground a moment later, watching the room spin before he hit the angled ceiling of the stairwell. He landed with a loud *crunch* on the second guardsman's pike, crumpling his ribcage and ripping the pike from the guard's hand.

The second guardsman only had time to curse before the first guardsman's pike speared him through the neck. The force sent him tumbling down the stone stairs. The Zealot charged after him, like a hawk diving on its prey.

The last two guardsmen spotted the Zealot as he rushed them, stepping off the wall at the top of the flight and leaping down with his knees tucked in front of him. The third guardsman lifted his pike to parry. The powerful Volgothan hit him like a battering ram, catching the pike pole in his hands and driving it back into the guard's throat. He hacked blood inside his helmet.

The Zealot clutched the choking guard's helmet by the eye holes. The stairway echoed with the smashing noise of the guards' two helmets together over and over again. Foam flecked off the corners of his mouth as he growled in rage. The Zealot, still clutching the third guardsman's helmet, bent it back at an unnatural angle. The stairway echoed with the loud *snap*.

His bared muscles dripped with sweat. He knelt and lifted the dead man's pike, baring his teeth in a snarl as he drove it down into the last crawling guardsman's back. He yanked the bent weapon free, and carried it with him to the armory.

~

Othric and Talla parted only as they heard Loesheron clamber quickly up the last flight of stairs. A bloody longsword was at his side. He sheathed it, brushed his messy black locks back, and cast a look behind himself.

"I had just donned my mail and cloak when they discovered me. I barred the gate, but that will not keep the guardsmen back for long." Turning to Talla, he held out a round helmet with vents dotted on the faceplate. "I could find nothing of your imperial armor, save for your helmet."

"Better than nothing," she clicked her tongue.

"May I?" he asked, lifting the helmet over his head.

Curiously, "Of course, sire. Indulge yourself."

Loesheron put on the helmet, nodding in thanks to her. Without another word, he pulled out a fist-sized glass globe filled with pulsing red potion and cast it back into his cell.

The cell ignited in a white fireball. The Zealot, turning his back to the blast, shielded the other two. Bits of flaming debris bounced off his helmet and cloak, which he spread out like great black wings around them. Every cage and chain rang in a terrible clamor, and the dungeon filled with dust and smoke.

Othric ambled over the scorched pebbles and shards of smoking iron. A few steps more, and he looked out a huge hole blown in the metal mesh. Below were the lights of the taverns and festival lanterns, and the sounds of music rising from the city.

"Quickly, you two first," Loesheron commanded, drawing out his longsword again. The guards would be there soon.

Othric lifted Talla in his arms, and recited an incantation both to her and the open air. Golden, shimmering strands appeared along his back, forming into a fine lattice shaped like two wings of a bird. The wings spread, and he plunged out the window with her clinging tightly to him.

The Zealot heard a noise behind him and instinctively drove his sword into the smoke. The dark blade dug into the unseen guardsman's belly. Stepping forward to the stairway, Loesheron kicked the guard off his blade and into the next one coming up behind him on the stairs.

He was about to charge the next attacker when an arrow glanced off the armor scales of his arm. Even his black suit of mail could not deflect a barrage of arrows.

The Zealot's luck had run out.

He ran for the cell and kicked the door shut behind him—anything that would give him an extra second. The guards were coming up the stairs now.

He searched for Othric but did not see him anywhere. He heard bow strings stretch behind him. The guards were at the cell door now.

He jumped.

Loesheron did not think of how the cold night air tore at his cloak or how it whistled through the vents of the helmet. He thought only of home.

Home.

He felt all the air expel from his lungs at the moment of collision, when the sorcerer tackled him around the waist to catch him. His wings leaving a bright trail like floating gold embers, Othric had thrown himself back skyward with all the speed he could muster. Talla, standing in the warm light of the lanterns nearby, watched breathlessly from the street. The two men soared downward as smoke rose from the scorched hole in the dungeon spire above them.

"She was right," Loesheron remarked to Othric as the two of them landed down beside Talla in the street below. "She knew you could do it."

Othric smiled at him, before doubling over with a yell of pain!

The Zealot caught him and immediately grimaced at the arrow stuck in Othric's back. He hardly had the chance to look up before more arrows rained down around them, one of them piercing the Zealot's shoulder pauldron. He growled. The two

Volgothans each took one of Othric's arms, dragging him out of the light and into the shadow between buildings. As they entered the alleyway, more arrows from the tower thunked loudly off the stone walls. Even more of them bristled out the ground behind them like grass.

"Steady, Othric, we've got you," Talla reassured him as she lowered him down deep in the alleyway. She stood and looked around. All around them was dark, cold stone. Nothing was in there but an old barrel. It would not add the height needed to vault over the walls, even if there were not archers waiting for them.

Loesheron knelt over the wounded man. "Keep calm, we're safe for the moment."

"We must... escape..." Othric moaned in pain, rolling to one side, and breathing hard.

"No, don't move—"

"Zealot please..." Othric grabbed Loesheron's arm. "Find any creeping thing... any creature you can."

Talla faltered, "Why do you—"

"Do it, please!" Othric shouted, sending her scrambling on her knees, searching the corners and crevices in the stone for a sleeping scavenger or some vermin...

And then she looked back at the barrel.

She threw it to its side and stomped it open, and a flurry of mice burst from where they nestled in the barrel's last stale morsels. Diving for them, she caught one and returned it to Othric.

"Will this do?" she panted. Her fingers held tightly to the tail of a small white mouse. Its red eyes were wide with fright as it squirmed and kicked its tiny legs.

He groaned, breathing hard. "Yes, well done, Talla..." and he began to recite an incantation.

The palace drawbridge dropped open with a loud crash, and dozens of guardsmen rushed out, barking at each other to find the escaped prisoners! Pikes and axes in hand, they rushed for the alley. The three lead guardsmen entered, weapons raised, with a flaming torch to light the way.

They flew backward, tumbling like ragdolls while their fellows dove for cover, for out of the alley roared a huge, powerful white pegasus with blood-red eyes! It snorted and shrieked angrily at the men, kicking and trampling them with its fur-tufted hooves. Spreading its wings, it launched itself up and into the night sky! The guardsmen scattered in the snow could only watch helplessly as the great flying beast carried away their three prisoners on its back.

~

The moon over Holireath was just a sliver, days away from the new moon. A white pegasus sailed across the cloudless sky all night.

Talla and Othric were as one, holding each other as they rode. For now, they simply had each other. They had needed nothing else since that day at the Black Shallows, when they fled breathlessly from a dark, cursed, corpse-littered shore. As soon as they were clear of Holireath and into the open country, they stopped to clean and dress Othric's wound. Fearing predators or ogres, they took flight again soon and stayed airborne all night.

Zealot Loesheron did not say a word until the violet glow of dawn was faint on the horizon.

"In the moment I leapt from the spire, I purposed in my heart where I wanted to go next," he said.

"Where's that, sire?" Talla asked.

"Back to Volgoth… where there are winding roads through the fields and the songs of children in the spring air. Where there are no patrolling sentinels in the streets, just old women feeding the geese. Where there is calm and hearth and home. Othric, come with us."

"Come with you?" the sorcerer's eyes widened.

Talla's ivory eyes shone with hope. "Yes! Let us away, we three, from these rogues and barbarians. Return with me to Volgoth!"

"Volgoth? B-but what fate awaits me there?"

Zealot Loesheron's black hair fluttered in the wind as he turned around. "You ask what fate, as a beast that knows not it can touch the sky… a humble creature who, with a gift bestowed, scattered warriors like frightened children. Let me bring you before the Ever-King himself, whose power is infinite, whose grace is limitless! To those who have lost their way, he gives new purpose!"

A smile crept onto Othric's face. He nodded.

"Your ancestors laid this path before you. They call you to something so much more. Once you were known as Othric the Great... but you could be something so much greater. Seed of Mirikinin... heir of destruction… come with me now, and I will kneel beside you at the throne of the immortal Ever-King."

Todd Mika (born 1985) is a fantasy writer based out of the American Midwest. As a young boy, he was captivated by classic literature: Longfellow's musings, Poe's madness, Tolstoy's lamentations, Dickens' tales, Shakespeare's sonnets, and Doyle's mysteries. By middle school he was penning heroic-fantasy game ideas and Star Wars fanfiction, which evolved into tabletop roleplaying games to play out his original stories with family and friends. In 2015, he self-published *Grimmgard*, an original roleplaying game book. Between sleepless nights writing new fiction, he enjoys exploring new coffee houses and experimenting with a variety of dangerous hot sauce.

Connect Online
https://www.grimmgard.com/
GrimmgardRPG@gmail.com

Made in the USA
Monee, IL
26 March 2021